'We may have to pretend for everyone else's sake that we are madly in love, but at least we can be honest with each other.'

'I thought we were being honest.' Marcus's voice was hard and cutting.

Gemma took a deep breath and launched in before she could change her mind. 'So I really think the decent thing would be for us to sleep in separate rooms.'

There was a moment's silence.

'You don't mean that?'

The arrogance of that remark made her angle her head up defiantly. 'Yes, I do.'

'We have an arrangement, Gemma. You are my wife and tonight we *will* consummate the marriage.'

D1081227

Kathryn Ross was born in Zambia, where her parents happened to live at that time. Educated in Ireland and England, she now lives in a village near Blackpool, Lancashire. Kathryn is a professional beauty therapist, but writing is her first love. As a child she wrote adventure stories, and at thirteen was editor of her school magazine. Happily, ten writing years later, DESIGNED WITH LOVE was accepted by Mills & Boon®. A romantic Sagittarian, she loves travelling to exotic locations.

Recent titles by the same author:

BLACKMAILED BY THE BOSS
THE SECRET CHILD
THE MILLIONAIRE'S AGENDA
HER DETERMINED HUSBAND

THE ITALIAN MARRIAGE

BY
KATHRYN ROSS

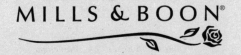
MILLS & BOON®

First published in Great Britain 2003
Harlequin Mills & Boon Limited,
Eton House, 18-24 Paradise Road, Richmond, Surrey TW9 1SR

© Kathryn Ross 2003

ISBN 0 263 83250 3

Set in Times Roman 10½ on 12 pt.
01-0703-49264

Printed and bound in Spain
by Litografia Rosés, S.A., Barcelona

CHAPTER ONE

'DADDY is getting married.'

The words fell in the drowsy heat of the summer afternoon like an incendiary device.

'Sorry?' Gemma had been pouring a glass of lemonade for her son and it spilt on the picnic rug, flowing over the hem of her floral sundress. 'What did you say, Liam?'

'You've spilt lemonade,' the four-year-old pointed out, reaching to get a chocolate bar from the picnic basket.

'Yes, I know.' Ordinarily, Gemma would have told her son not to eat the chocolate until he'd finished his sandwiches but her mind was in total disarray. 'What did you say about Daddy?' she asked again, trying hard not to sound flustered.

'He's going to get married.' Liam munched on the chocolate and regarded her steadily from dark eyes that were unnervingly like his father's. 'Does that mean I will have two mummys like Annie does?'

'Well…I suppose it does…'

Gemma was at a loss to know what to say. She was still reeling with shock.

It was strange how one moment the world could seem settled and then the next a gaping great hole could open up under your feet. She didn't know why she felt so shocked…or surprised. Marcus Rossini was thirty-eight, spectacularly handsome, and wealthy. He'd had his pick of women for years. With forty looming on the horizon, maybe he thought it was finally time to put his philandering days behind him and settle down.

So who was the woman? she wondered. She'd put bets on it being his childhood sweetheart, Sophia Albani. Women had come and gone over the years but she seemed to have remained in the background—despite the miles that sometimes separated them, despite the fact that Marcus had fathered a child. Sophia had taken it all in her stride and their relationship seemed to have survived, against all odds. Maybe that was the test of true love? For some reason the pain of that thought seared straight through to Gemma's heart.

'Are you sure about this, Liam?' she asked her son gently. 'How do you know Daddy is getting married? Did he tell you himself?'

Liam shook his head and reached into the basket to get a biscuit. 'I was supposed to be in bed but I got up because I had tummy ache and I heard him talking…'

'Was this last night?'

Liam nodded.

Curiosity ate into Gemma. 'Who was he talking to?'

Liam shrugged.

'Do you think it was Sophia? Was she at Daddy's house yesterday?'

'He was talking on the phone.' Liam grasped a packet of crisps and Gemma broke from the trance that had possessed her. Interrogating a four-year-old was not the done thing and Marcus's personal life was nothing to do with her.

'Liam, no more junk food. Eat a sandwich, please.'

Liam wrinkled his nose. 'I don't like them. I don't like that green squishy stuff.'

'It's not squishy, it's cucumber and you love it.'

Liam shook his head mutinously. 'I hate it.'

'Just have one to please me.'

'Daddy doesn't make me eat horrid things.'

Gemma felt a flash of irritation. It was always the same. Liam idolized his dad; she felt that she heard a sentence similar to this half a million times during the day. 'Daddy doesn't make me go to bed this early…Daddy lets me watch this programme on TV…Daddy reads to me when I wake up at night…'

Gemma tried to let it all go over her head without resorting to any sarcastic replies, but sometimes when she was tired or harassed it was more than flesh and blood could stand and she really wanted to say something derogatory—something that would tell Liam that his wonderful daddy wasn't a man you could trust.

But of course she would never, never stoop that low. Because the truth of the matter was that, no matter how much Marcus Rossini had hurt her in the past, or how much she wanted to forget his very existence, he was a damned good dad to Liam and that was all that really counted in the end.

'Please don't argue with me, Liam. Just eat the sandwich. Otherwise I just might have to tell Daddy that you've been naughty when he comes to pick you up tonight.'

She watched as the child hesitated and then dutifully did as he was asked. It always worked, Gemma thought, as she dabbed at the hem of her dress with a tissue to mop up the lemonade. And the irony was that her conversations with his father were as brief as Gemma could possibly make them. She never discussed anything with him except the arrangements for picking Liam up. In fact, she hadn't even seen Marcus for months, because as soon as his car drew up outside she sent Liam out with his bag ready packed, eliminating the need for

Marcus even to walk through her front door. And, when he returned, she had her mother answer the door to them. Gemma found it easier that way. She couldn't converse easily with Marcus—not without reopening lots of old wounds.

Thankfully, Liam was too young to realize this at the moment, but one day, she supposed, the threat of reporting him to his dad wouldn't work quite so easily.

Was Marcus really going to get married? she wondered as she watched Liam. She felt something inside her twist painfully. Not that she cared on a personal level, she told herself firmly; she had long ago resigned herself to the fact that Marcus was not the man for her. She was only concerned about how it would affect Liam.

'Can I go on the swings now?' Liam asked as he finished his sandwich.

'Yes, if you like.'

She watched as he ran the short distance towards the playground, little legs hurtling along in blue jeans like a mini tornado. Then he turned around halfway there and ran back to her, flinging his arms around her and kissing her on the cheek. 'I love you, Mummy,' he said.

'I love you too,' Gemma said, giving him a hug.

'Will you watch how high I can go on the swings?' His dark eyes were filled with an impish excitement.

'I will, darling.'

She watched as he ran off into the playground again, her heart heavy with pride and with love.

Although it was a sunny Saturday afternoon there weren't many people in the park. If it wasn't for the distant roar of the London traffic they could have pretended they were in the midst of the countryside.

Gemma wondered what Marcus was doing today. He usually picked Liam up in the morning and spent the weekend with him, but there had been a last-minute change of plan. He'd had the boy last night instead, dropping him off early this morning, because he said he had something to do today and that he would pick him up again around four-thirty.

Maybe he was seeing Sophia…maybe he was taking her out today to buy an engagement ring?

Gemma put the box of sandwiches away into the basket and settled back on the blanket to watch her son. Marcus could set up a harem for all she cared, she told herself briskly. It was none of her business.

The drone of bees plundering the foxgloves in the flowerbed next to her filled the air. For a second the heat and the tranquillity conjured up the memory of an afternoon when she had lain entwined in Marcus's arms by the banks of a river. His hands had been running possessively and confidently over her body, finding the buttons of her blouse and stealing beneath the material to find the heat of her naked flesh. 'I want to make love to you, Gemma…I want you right now…'

The heat and the urgency of that memory made her go hot inside now, with a renewed surge of longing. And she hated herself for it. It was years since she had slept with Marcus and those feelings were dead, she told herself fiercely. Dead and buried, with a full grieving process very firmly behind her.

'Hi, Gemma.' Marcus's voice coming so coolly and so quickly on top of the steamy memory made her sit bolt upright and turn around.

It was almost as if she had conjured him up, as if he had stepped out from her daydreams and into reality.

'What are you doing here?' she asked in stunned surprise.

'I've come to see you.' He sat down beside her on

the rug, his manner relaxed and confident, as if they always met like this on a Saturday afternoon in the park.

'Liam told me you were coming here today for a picnic.'

'Did he…?' Gemma could hardly concentrate for thinking how attractive he looked. Marcus was half Italian and he had dark Latin smouldering good looks, olive skin and jet-black hair that gleamed almost blue in the sunlight. Blue chinos and a faded blue shirt sat well on the tall broad-shouldered frame.

Every time Gemma saw him she was struck afresh by how gorgeous he was, and she could remember forcibly what it was that had drawn her so firmly under his spell in the first place. There was something very powerful about Marcus Rossini and it wasn't just that his body was well-toned and muscular. It was everything about him; the set of his jaw, the chiselled, strong profile and the gleam of his velvet dark eyes. As those eyes held hers now, Gemma felt a shiver of apprehension.

'You look well,' he said politely.

'Thanks.'

'Seems ages since I saw you.'

She felt his eyes running in a quick assessment over her long blonde hair and slender figure; felt them as acutely as if he were touching her and it stirred up a renewed feeling of heat inside her. And suddenly she knew why she was so careful to avoid contact with this man. There was something about him that could stir her senses with just a glance.

'So what do you want, Marcus?' Her voice was sharper than she intended but he didn't appear to notice.

'There is something I need to discuss with you,' he said calmly.

Gemma remained silent; she knew what was coming. He was going to tell her he was getting married. She was surprised he had bothered to come and tell her in person. She supposed it was decent of him…supposed it was the civilized way to proceed. After all, they had a duty to their son to handle this in an adult way. Trouble was, she suddenly wasn't feeling at all civilized.

Gemma took a deep breath and tried to prepare herself to react appropriately. She would wish him well and sound as if she meant it.

As their eyes met she felt her heart slam against her chest. Suddenly from nowhere she was remembering the night she had told him she was pregnant, and her feelings when he had proposed. She had felt the same heavy weight of emotion pressing against her chest then. The need to cry, to wail against the unfairness of the fact that this man just didn't love her and would never love her. She had been left with no option but to turn him down. A marriage without love was no marriage at all.

Now he was about to tell her he was marrying someone else. There was a bitter taste at the back of her throat.

She looked away from him over towards Liam. He was swinging higher and higher, a look of intense concentration on his face, and he hadn't even noticed that his dad was here yet.

'I'm leaving London, Gemma,' Marcus said quietly beside her. 'I'm going back to live in Italy and I want to take Liam with me.'

Gemma stared at him blankly, shock waves pounding through her. This wasn't at all what she had expected.

'I know this is a shock, but when you calm down and think about it rationally you'll realize this is a sensible move. This is the best thing for Liam. He is part Italian, he has a heritage and a way of life to learn about. He has the security of a large family waiting for him—cousins, uncles, aunts, not to mention a grandfather who loves him deeply.'

Gemma didn't know why she was allowing Marcus to continue with this conversation. It was quite frankly crazy, but she was so shocked she couldn't find her voice to stop him.

'Liam belongs back home in Italy.'

'Liam's home is here with me.' When she finally managed to speak, her voice was so full of anger that it didn't even sound like her.

'I understand this is going to be a wrench for you Gemma.'

With a fierce stab of panic Gemma noticed that he spoke as if this was already a fait accompli.

'And I know how much you love Liam. That's why I think you and I should get together on this and sort out a compromise that will suit us all.'

'It's not going to be a wrench because it will never happen.' She cut across his calm words with a fierce determination and started to pack away the bottle of lemonade and the cups, needing to get away from this situation as quickly as she could.

He watched her frantic, angry movements with a cool detachment.

'Look, I suggest that we put our own feelings aside and concentrate on what's best for Liam now.'

The sheer arrogance of those words made Gemma look sharply up at him. 'I have always concentrated on what is best for Liam,' she said furiously, her blue eyes blazing with emotion. 'How dare you suggest otherwise?'

'Gemma, all I'm saying—'

'I hear what you're saying and you are talking rubbish. You waltz in at weekends and high days and holidays and think you are God's gift to fatherhood. Well, let me tell you that you're not. You have no idea of the day-to-day reality of being a parent. This idea is just a passing fancy...like everything else in your life.'

She couldn't resist the sarcastic dig. 'And you wouldn't last two minutes if you had Liam full time.'

'Well, that's where I think you are wrong. I would be more than capable of having Liam full time.'

She noticed that his voice had lost the cool, pragmatic tone and there was an edge of annoyance showing now. Good, she thought furiously. How dared he calmly arrive and tell her he intended to take her son away? 'No judge in the land would take a baby away from his mother without extreme good cause,' she added tersely. 'So just go away, Marcus. Go back to your dream world and don't bother me again.'

'He's not a baby, Gemma. He will be starting school in September.'

Gemma ignored the comment and continued to tidy away the chocolate wrappers from the rug.

As she reached to fasten the lid on the basket Marcus stretched out and caught hold of her wrist. The contact of his skin against hers sent a jolt of shock shooting through her as if an electric charge had passed through her body. 'This is something we need to sort out together. If it goes to court you will regret it, Gemma.'

Although the words were softly spoken the meaning was clear. Nobody took on the might of the Rossini family and won. They had money and influence and they always got what they wanted. Gemma tried very hard not to let panic show in her eyes as she looked over at him. 'You are not in Italy now, Marcus,' she reminded him. 'This is my home turf, and a court will never allow you to take Liam away from me.'

'I don't want to fight with you, Gemma,' he said softly. 'But if you insist on it, then I will use any means possible to make sure I win. If you play with fire then you must expect to be burnt.'

'Daddy!' Liam's excited voice cut through the tense atmosphere and Marcus let go of her and turned as the little boy came running across the grass and flung himself into his arms.

Gemma watched the instinctive way Liam curled his arms around his father's neck, cuddling in to him as close as he could get. 'Daddy, will you push me on the swing? Will you? I can go really high, almost up to the sky and…'

'Hey, steady on, partner.' Marcus laughed. 'Give me time to draw breath.'

'Liam, we have to go now,' Gemma cut in anxiously. She just wanted to be away from this situation. Her nerves couldn't stand being around Marcus a moment longer.

'Ah, Mum!' Liam groaned. 'Daddy's only just come! Can't he push me on the swings, can't he, please?'

'You can see him later.' Gemma stood up and pretended to busy herself brushing down the folds of her long dress. 'You're spending tonight over at Daddy's house. You can play on the swing in his garden.'

Marcus watched the way her long hair fell silkily over her shoulders, gleaming a rich honey gold in the sun; noticed the deep V of her sundress revealing a tantalizing glimpse of her curvaceous body.

'Can I stay here with Daddy?'

The words caused a sharp rush of pain inside her.

'No, you can't.' Gemma glanced over and met Marcus's eyes. She imagined there was a gleam of triumph in them, a look that said, See, my son wants to be with me, not you. 'Please stand up from the rug so I can fold it away,' she asked him coldly.

Liam seemed set to argue some more. But, surprisingly, Marcus cut across him. 'Do as Mummy says, Liam,' he said, getting to his feet and lifting Liam with him so that Gemma could pack the rug away.

'Thanks.' Her voice was prickly.

'We need to talk some more,' Marcus said quietly as he watched her place the folded blanket over the top of the basket.

'There is nothing to discuss. I've given you my answer.'

'That's not good enough.'

'Why? Because it isn't the answer you want?' Gemma shrugged. 'Well, tough, Marcus. I know you are used to getting your own way, but not this time.'

Anger glimmered in Marcus's eyes. 'We'll see about that.'

The quiet way he said those words disturbed the cool veneer she had managed to wrap around herself. 'The whole notion is ridiculous, Marcus, so just forget it.'

As her voice rose, Liam looked over at her. 'Are you and Daddy arguing?'

'No, darling, we're just talking.' Gemma held out her hand to him. 'Come on, we have to get home. Uncle Richard said he might call.'

Marcus felt a flash of annoyance at that remark. 'Uncle Richard' was around at the house far too much recently for his liking.

'We'll talk again later in the week,' Marcus said as he put Liam down.

'I told you, there's nothing to talk about.'

'On the contrary, there is a lot to talk about,' Marcus

said coolly. 'How about having dinner with me next Friday night? Will your mother babysit?'

'Dinner?' Gemma looked at him as if he'd gone mad. 'No, she wouldn't.'

'Okay, I'll come over to you, then.'

'Marcus, that isn't convenient.'

'I'll ring you later in the week to confirm.' Marcus's voice was steely.

Gemma was going to tell him flatly not to waste his time but Liam was watching and listening intently. So she just reached to take hold of the child's hand. 'Goodbye, Marcus,' she said with as much cold finality in her voice as she could muster.

Marcus watched as she walked away from him across the grass, her long hair swinging glossily behind her in the softness of the breeze, her back ramrod straight.

Liam was skipping beside her and kept turning to wave at him but Gemma did not look back.

But she would do as he wanted, Marcus told himself grimly. By the time he had finished she would be begging him to compromise and he would have her exactly where he wanted her: back in his life.

CHAPTER TWO

GEMMA groaned and put the letter down on the table, pulling a hand distractedly through her long hair. 'This is all I need!'

'What's the matter?' Her mother walked into the kitchen just at that moment. 'It's not a letter from Marcus's lawyer, is it? This custody battle isn't going to court?'

'No!' Gemma looked over at her mother, horrified by the words. 'There is no custody battle, Mum. Marcus is trying his luck, that's all. He won't dare go to court because he knows he'll lose.'

Her mother didn't look convinced. 'Marcus has never struck me as a man afraid of losing,' she said curtly.

The words were not what Gemma needed to hear. She was desperately trying to convince herself that this problem with Marcus would sort itself out, that he would change his mind before things started to get nasty.

'What's in the letter?' her mother asked now.

'It's from the letting agency, informing me that the landlord is putting this house up for sale. They've invited me to make an offer, as he will give me first refusal, apparently.'

'Would you be able to afford it?'

'They haven't said how much he wants for it, but I doubt it. The houses in this square are going for a fortune these days.'

'I suppose you've done well getting it for such a low rent for all these years. I don't know how you've managed it. Your friend Jane is paying twice as much for her small flat.'

'Yes, I suppose it was too good to last.' Gemma had thought her luck was really in when she had found this place. It was a large Georgian house close to her publishing job in the heart of London and within walking distance of her mother's house. Fully furnished with the most exquisite antiques, there was even a large office where she could work. The rent had been preposterously low but apparently the landlord's main concern was to have a good tenant who would look after the property, as it had once been his mother's home. 'I thought he might bump up the rent one day but somehow I didn't expect him to sell,' Gemma reflected sadly.

She watched as her mother lifted the letter and shook her head in dismay. 'Maybe you could ask Marcus for some help to buy the place,' she suggested tentatively. 'I'm sure he would—'

'No, Mum.' Gemma turned and opened the kitchen door to call up the stairs to Liam. 'Liam, your nana is here to take you to nursery.'

'A house like this would be nothing to a man of Marcus's wealth and he is always offering you financial assistance,' her mother continued determinedly as if Gemma had said nothing. 'I don't know why you keep turning him down. You're so damn stubborn sometimes—'

'Mum, I am not going to ask Marcus for help.' Gemma put on the jacket of her smart black business suit and checked her keys were in her bag. She was running late and she had a stressful day at work ahead of her: she didn't want to think about Marcus, let alone talk about him. 'He's the man who wants to take Liam away from me, remember? The last thing I'll do is go to him cap in hand.'

'It doesn't need to be like that. Marcus is a decent enough man, and I'm sure—'

'You can't be sure of anything where Marcus is concerned. And I don't need his help. I'll manage,' Gemma said positively before going out into the hall to call upstairs again. 'Liam, Mummy will be late for work.'

Joanne Hampton followed her daughter out into the hall. 'How will you manage?' she persisted. 'The cost of living in London is going through the roof, Gemma. You have to be practical. It's hard being a single parent.'

'I've got a good job, Mum,' Gemma reminded her patiently. 'And I'm in line for promotion again. If I get this new job, who knows, maybe I will be able to put in a bid for this house.' As she spoke she swallowed down nervous anticipation. She did have a good job and her career had been going from strength to strength over these last few years. She had worked her way through the various editorial departments of *Modern Times*, a glossy monthly magazine, and had been made deputy editor last year. Now she was up for consideration for editor because Susan Kershaw, the present editor, was leaving.

Everyone said she stood a very good chance of getting the top job. She was talented and she was driven. Even Gemma was quite confident that she could outperform the competition. Circulation of the magazine was up and she had more than proven herself over the last year. In fact, she had been feeling quite relaxed about the whole thing until rumours of a take-over bid for the magazine had started a few weeks ago. And suddenly her rosy picture for the future had developed a few disturbing black clouds.

No one was certain who had made the take-over bid, but if it was successful there might be redundancies. The first to go would be the top jobs, as the new company were likely to want to put their own key people in.

But even if she lost her job she would walk into another one, she told herself confidently. She had a great CV.

All right, maybe she wouldn't earn enough to buy a house as beautiful and in such a good area as this, but she could afford to rent something decent around here. And as long as she maintained her independence and a nice way of life for Liam, that was all that mattered.

Gemma glanced towards the stairs again. 'Liam, I'm going to come up in a minute,' she warned.

'What's he doing up there?' her mother asked.

'Playing with a train set Marcus bought for him last week. The tracks are all the way around his bed.'

Joanne smiled. 'He's a good man. Gemma, why don't you go out for dinner with him tomorrow night. I've been thinking about it and the pair of you should sit down and talk about Liam's future, work this custody matter out. I'll babysit for you.'

'There's nothing to work out,' Gemma insisted. Marcus had rung several times that week and had left messages on her machine, but she hadn't called him back and she wasn't going to. 'Marcus has my answer and that's the end of it.'

'Nevertheless, you need to talk to him about it, soften your attitude.'

'Soften my attitude!' Gemma looked at her mother in consternation. 'If I do that he'll walk away with my son, and that will be that.'

'Marcus is a reasonable man. I'm sure you can come to some compromise.'

'Not over this.' Gemma shook her head firmly. She wished her mother wouldn't always talk so positively about Marcus. She never tried to hide the fact that she thought he was wonderful and at every opportunity she thrust the fact at Gemma. Over the years Gemma had got used to it and accepted it. But given the circumstances, the fact that Marcus wanted to take Liam away, she would have thought her mother might be seeing things a little more from her side at the moment. It was disturbing that she wasn't—hurtful, even.

'Do you think Liam is right and Marcus is getting married?' her mother asked suddenly. 'Maybe he's settling down with that Italian girl. What's she called? Sophia? Maybe that's why he's moving back there.'

'Maybe.' That thought had already tormented Gemma through several long sleepless nights. 'But, whatever the reason, he is not having Liam.'

Gemma was relieved when Liam appeared at the top of the stairs, bringing the conversation to a close.

As he hurried down to stand beside them, Gemma noticed he looked a little flushed. 'Are you okay, darling?' she asked, bending to put one hand on his forehead.

His skin felt clammy under the coolness of her hand. 'Are you feeling ill?'

'I'm okay.' Liam shrugged.

'He's probably been racing around after that train,' his grandmother said with a laugh.

'I've built tunnels under the bed and a big loop by the bathroom door,' Liam said with a grin. 'Come and look, Nana.'

'Maybe later.' Joanne smiled. 'We have to go now. Otherwise, Mummy will be late for work and I'll be late for my bridge club.'

*   *   *

Thank heavens Liam hadn't been ill this morning, Gemma thought, as she sat at her desk half an hour later and dealt with a mountain of paperwork. If she'd had to have today off it could have been disastrous. The office was chaotic and a lot of the top executives were huddled together in the boardroom, giving a sense of urgency to everything.

'They're calling a meeting later.' Richard Barry, the new features editor of the magazine, paused by her desk on the way to get himself a coffee. 'Looks like the take-over is going through after all.'

Gemma felt slightly ill at those words. If that was the case, it was likely that all her hard work for the job of editor wouldn't pay off.

'Hey, don't look so worried.' Richard perched on the edge of her desk for a moment. 'You are one of the most talented editors I've ever worked with, you'll get your job.'

'Thanks for the vote of confidence, Richard, but I doubt it.' She smiled up at him. Richard was an attractive man and he had become a close personal friend over the last couple of months. She really liked him. Liked him more, perhaps, than any other man she had met in the last few years.

'Shall I get you a coffee from the machine to cheer you up?' he asked now.

Gemma laughed at that. The coffee from the machine was so bad that it had become a standing office joke. It was said that anyone who wanted to end it all only had to overindulge by a few cups to achieve their aim. 'Go on, then. I'll live dangerously, thanks.'

As Richard left her office she watched him through the glass walls of her office. She had one of the few private offices on the floor but her door was always open and the glass walls made her feel part of what was going on out in the main body. Now she noticed there was a stir up by the reception area, and as she glanced over she saw with a shock that Marcus Rossini had just stepped out of the lift.

The nerve of the man, she thought furiously. How dared he come to confront her at work? She watched with a small gleam of satisfaction, knowing that if he didn't have an appointment, Clare, the receptionist, would not let him in without gaining clearance from her first…clearance she had no intention of giving. Marcus could get lost.

She waited for the phone on her desk to ring, but instead, a few minutes later, Gemma watched incredulously as Marcus strode on in through the office in the direction of her desk. What the hell had he said to Clare? she wondered. Probably turned on that fabulous Italian charm of his, or maybe he had merely smiled. She noticed the effect he was having on the other women out in the office as he walked past them: they were all looking at him with ill-disguised appreciation. It was always the same, Gemma thought with annoyance, women just fell at Marcus's feet. But not her, she thought grimly. She was older and wiser now and knew the dangers of that particular pitfall.

She had to admit, though, he did look good. The dark business suit did incredible things for an already very desirable physique. Annoyed with herself for allowing that thought to cross her mind, she glared at him as he strolled nonchalantly into her office.

'What on earth do you want?' she asked sharply. 'Because I'm telling you now, Marcus, I haven't got time for whatever it is.'

'That's hardly a congenial welcome, Gemma,' he chastised softly.

'That's because I'm not feeling particularly congenial where you are concerned.' She felt a tremor of apprehension as he shut the door behind him, closing her into the confined space with him. 'That door always remains open,' she told him, but he ignored her completely and left it closed, taking a seat in the chair at the other side of her desk.

He looked extremely relaxed and yet more formidable than ever, his expression as businesslike and serious as his clothing.

'Clare shouldn't have allowed you in here,' Gemma said heatedly. 'In case you hadn't noticed, I'm trying to work and this isn't a convenient time.'

'Unfortunately, there never seems to be a convenient time, does there, Gemma? As you have not returned any of my calls, you've left me no option but to come in here to sort things out in person.'

She didn't like the sound of that at all. It made a nervous flutter start in the base of her stomach. 'Marcus, I have nothing to say to you, and I want you to leave now.'

As he made no effort to move she continued in a more heated tone. 'Look, I've asked you nicely, but if you continue to refuse you'll leave me no option but to ring through for Security to remove you.'

Far from seeming worried by that, he looked slightly amused. 'I never realized before what a fighter you are, Gemma,' he murmured. 'But I have to warn you that if you take such an action, you might get more than you bargained for. You might find that you are the one who is removed from the office.'

Gemma shook her head contemptuously. 'Your arrogance never ceases to amaze me, Marcus. You may have been able to charm your way around the receptionist, but two burly security guards will be a different matter.'

'Why haven't you returned my phone calls?' he asked, totally ignoring that.

'You know why.'

'You've been working day and night for the last few days?' he said sardonically. 'When I dropped Liam back on Sunday your mother told me you were working. And I've left several messages on your answering machine now, the first on Sunday evening, the last yesterday morning.'

'I've been busy.'

'Too busy to make time to discuss our son's future?'

The nonchalant question fired her blood. 'There is nothing further to discuss.'

He didn't answer that. 'Nice office you've got here,' he remarked instead. 'And I hear you're looking to move even higher within the company.'

'How do you know that?'

'You seem to forget that I'm a player in the publishing world myself. Let's say I've got my ear to the ground.'

If ever there was an understatement, it was that. Marcus didn't just 'play' at publishing: he ran one of the largest companies in Europe. Rossini House was massive; it owned some of the most well respected publishing firms in the business. *Modern Times* was very small fry compared to anything Marcus ran or was remotely interested in.

'Well, I'm flattered that you're taking such an interest in my career,' she replied sardonically. 'Obviously, you have a lot of spare time on your hands. Or is life just incredibly dull for you at the moment?'

'Life's pretty good, Gemma. Thank you for your concern,' he replied smoothly, completely ignoring her sarcasm. 'So what do you think your chances are of getting this promotion?'

'I don't know…I suppose I'm quietly confident.' She frowned, wondering why he was asking her this.

'If I remember rightly, you're not bad at your job,' he reflected.

'Not bad?' Her frown deepened. 'Actually, I'm damn good at my job, as you well know. It's the reason I was offered a job all those years ago at one of your companies.'

He regarded her steadily for a moment as if she were a piece of artwork he was thinking of buying. Her blonde hair was tied back in a schoolgirl ponytail, which showed the perfect proportions of her face, the high cheekbones, the soft, sensual curve of her lips, the large, vivid blue eyes. She wore light make-up but she didn't need any; her skin was flawless and creamy.

Her body was still ripe perfection.

At twenty-nine, Gemma had hardly changed since the day she had first walked into his office five and a half years ago. 'Your work wasn't the only reason you were offered a job,' he said with soft emphasis, then smiled as he saw a bright flush of colour light her skin.

'I'm sure you haven't come here to reminisce about old times, or ask about my work, so perhaps you had better just get to the point,' she said, annoyed with herself for allowing that remark to unsettle her.

'I think you know what the point is,' he said quietly.

'Liam is not going to live with you in Italy, so you may as well just give up on the idea and go away.'

'Giving up isn't an option, Gemma.'

She glanced beyond him towards the main office. People were looking over at them; curiosity was obviously rife out there. 'You are causing a scene, Marcus, and I want you to go.'

'Not until you've agreed to come out for dinner with me tomorrow.'

'I can't—'

'Your mother informed me that she would gladly babysit for us, so what time shall I pick you up?'

'Watch my lips, Marcus. I will not go out with you tomorrow. And where Liam lives is not up for discussion. He is staying with me.'

'I'll book a table at Bellingham's for seven-thirty. How does that suit?'

'You can get a table at Buckingham Palace for all I care. I still won't be there.'

Why was he being so insistent about taking her out for dinner? she wondered furiously. Did he think that was the best place to tell her he was planning to get married? Gemma shivered at the thought…that was a bit too civilized for her taste.

She tried to return her attention to her work, to pretend he wasn't there. And hoped he would just get the message and leave.

'Is it always going to be like this between us?'

The softly spoken question made her look up. 'Like what?' she asked, puzzled.

'Guns drawn at twenty paces.' He gave a small smile.

'That's not fair, Marcus. I have always been very co-operative with you. I've let you see Liam whenever you want. Even at very short notice, I change my plans to fit in with your work schedule. I think I've been more than helpful—'

'What about the fact that I don't agree with the school you are sending him to in September?' Marcus cut across her suddenly.

She frowned, the remark taking her by surprise. 'There's nothing wrong with that school. It's close by—'

'I don't like it.'

'What do you mean, you don't like it? What would you know about it?' she asked impatiently.

'I just think we could send him somewhere better.'

'You mean to a school with colossal fees?' She shook her head angrily. 'Just because a school costs a lot doesn't—'

'That's not what I mean at all, Gemma.'

'So what do you mean?' she asked, and then promptly wished she hadn't when she noticed the smile of satisfaction on Marcus's face.

'You see, we do have things to discuss.'

'Discussing local schools is a very different proposition to discussing taking Liam out of the country completely,' she said quickly.

'Yes, but up to two minutes ago you didn't even want to discuss local schools,' Marcus pointed out coolly.

He was right; she didn't. The simple fact was that she was scared of Marcus taking over completely. It was in the nature of the man: he was arrogant, and he was powerful. If she gave him even an inch he would take the whole nine yards. He thought he could say and have anything he wanted…and maybe he could, maybe that was really what scared her. He had always had the strangest effect on her. Just sitting this close to him across the desk made her heart rate increase, made her whole body turn to red alert. Having sensible, unemotional talks with Marcus was something she was incapable of doing.

'I just want to be more involved in my son's upbringing, Gemma. Is that such a bad thing?'

Gemma stared at him in exasperation. She couldn't honestly say that it was.

'But you don't let me help you in any way—'

'If you're going to start talking about money, you can forget it, Marcus. We have been all through this subject before and I've told you I don't want or need your help. I'm managing perfectly well by myself, and that's how I like it.'

She saw his face tighten, saw the flare of annoyance in his dark eyes, but she held his gaze with determination. She was resolute on this, because she knew if she handed over the financial reins to him he would really have a hold over her.

'And don't worry about the school,' she continued hurriedly. 'It will be good for Liam. My friend's little girl, Annie, goes there as well, so he will feel right at home,' she continued firmly.

'Oh, well, if Annie goes there it must be fine,' Marcus grated sarcastically. 'To hell with academic achievement.'

'He's four years of age, Marcus. He can train to be a brain surgeon a little later on,' she retorted with equal sarcasm. 'My main priority at the moment is that he's happy.'

'If that's the case, then come out for dinner with me tomorrow night.'

'So we can fight between courses. I don't think so. Liam is not going to Italy, he is staying here with me, and he is going to a local school.' She glanced beyond him towards the office again. There was a sense of unreality about being closeted in here with Marcus discussing schools of all things on a stressful Thursday with deadlines looming and chaos reigning in the boardroom. The day had started on a bad note and seemed to be going rapidly downhill. She wondered if it could get any worse.

'You are the most stubborn woman I have ever met, do you know that?' Marcus said quietly.

Gemma noticed Henry Perkins, the company director, coming out of the boardroom to get himself a coffee from the machine. He looked as stressed as she felt, she noted. Although he was a relatively young man at forty-five he seemed to have aged ten years in the last few weeks.

'The fact remains that, no matter what you say to the contrary, Liam is a very happy child.' She returned her attention to Marcus. 'He's well adjusted and secure, and I want to make sure things stay like that. And anyway, maybe if you cared a little more about Liam and a little less about yourself, you wouldn't be thinking of leaving him and going to live in Italy.'

She knew she had scored a bulls-eye with that remark as she saw his face darken angrily. He wasn't the only one who could use emotional blackmail to get what he wanted, she thought with satisfaction.

'Things aren't that black and white,' he said crossly.

'They never are.' She hesitated before asking curiously, 'So what's drawing you back to Italy? Some nubile woman waiting in the wings, I take it. Or are you finally going to make an honest woman of Sophia?'

There was a moment's silence, then Marcus grinned. 'Hell, Gemma, you sound almost jealous.'

'Don't be ridiculous.' She wished she hadn't asked now, wished she had contained both her curiosity and the barbed comment. 'On the contrary, I hope you will be very happy.'

'Thank you.'

Was that all he was going to say? Was he not going

to enlighten her at all? She stared at him in frustration, wanting to ask him more but not daring to in case he thought she really was jealous…which, of course, she wasn't, just consumed with curiosity.

'So, while we are on this new and enlightened ''be nice to each other'' path, how about agreeing to have dinner with me tomorrow night?'

'The answer is still no, Marcus. Now we've had our conversation, and I want you to go. I'm stressed enough at the moment without you coming in here making trouble.'

'What are you stressed about?' he asked calmly.

For a second she contemplated telling him about the rumoured take-over bid for the magazine, then decided the less he knew about the details of her financial life the better. 'Let's just say that today is not the best of days in this office, and your presence here is making matters worse.' She glanced up, noticed Richard hovering outside the door with her coffee and waved him in, in the hope that Marcus would go once someone else was present.

As the door opened Marcus glanced coolly around. 'Wait outside, will you?' he said to a startled Richard, who had only taken a step inside. 'We are having a private conversation.'

'Oh, right you are.' To Gemma's annoyance, Richard immediately retreated and closed the door again.

'How dare you talk to Richard like that?' she flared angrily. 'He's the features editor, not one of your lackeys.'

'I don't care who he is. Richard can wait,' Marcus ground out tersely.

She glared at him.

'You think you can manage very well on your own,

Gemma, but you are being naïve. It's hard being a single parent—'

'I know it's hard. You're preaching to the converted, Marcus. It's you who has no idea of reality. Now, if you don't mind, I have a living to make and a son to support.'

His eyes narrowed. 'I know you like to think of yourself as very independent, but believe me, without my support you would find things very tough…very tough indeed.'

The quietly spoken words puzzled her. 'I don't need any support from you, Marcus. I never have and I never will.'

'Really?' Marcus rose from his chair, his manner very cool suddenly. 'Such big words…let's hope you're not speaking rashly, Gemma. Because, from what I hear, your life is in a state of flux at the moment.'

'What do you mean?'

'Well, for one thing, I hear that the house you are renting is up for sale,' he said casually.

'How do you know about that?' She stared up at him in confusion and then the mist cleared. Obviously, her mother had contacted him this morning, had gone ahead and asked for his help. Was that why he had rushed around here now, because he thought he could use this to his advantage? Furiously she shook her head. 'Look, Marcus, I don't know what Mum has told you, but…'

'Your mother hasn't told me anything.'

'So how do you know the house is for sale? It hasn't even gone on the market yet.'

He leaned on the back of the chair and stared at her, a wry look on his face as he watched her perplexity. 'Oh, come on, Gemma, you didn't honestly think you could rent a house like that for what you've been paying?'

'You mean you've been paying my rent?' She struggled blindly to comprehend what was going on here.

'I've waived your rent,' he said nonchalantly. 'The house belongs to me. You see, I know you have been determined not to accept my help in any way but I have been doubly determined that you should.'

'Well, you had no right!' All colour drained from her skin and she stood up to face him on legs that were decidedly shaky. 'I told you I didn't want you interfering in my life—'

'I wasn't interfering and I didn't do it for you, I did it for my son,' he said calmly.

'And now, when it suits, you're throwing us out…' Her tone was icily cold. 'And you wonder why I didn't want to accept any help from you in the first place.'

'I'm not throwing you out. You can continue to live there for as long as you like. I'm just giving you a wake-up call. I've tried to tell you nicely, now I'm telling you clearly. I won't allow you to shut me out of Liam's life for a moment longer.'

'Well, here's a wake-up call for you,' Gemma retorted furiously. 'I wouldn't want to live in that house now if it was the last one left standing in London. Liam and I will be moving out at the end of the month.'

'When Liam moves out of that house he will be accompanying me back to Italy,' Marcus replied calmly.

'Not while there is a single ounce of strength left in my body.'

Marcus walked slowly around the desk until he was standing very close to her, then reached out and touched her face. Considering the fact that they were both intensely angry it was a strangely tender caress and it made her shiver deep inside. 'I can think of better ways for that beautiful body of yours to expend energy,' he murmured.

Her eyes locked with his and she felt her breathing quickening, her pulses racing in disarray. She tried to tell herself to move back from him, but it was as if he held her under some kind of spell and she was unable to break free. Her body was a whisper breath from his and she felt the electric magnetism of him invade her very soul.

'I don't want to fight with you, Gemma. We both have Liam's best interests at heart,' he continued softly. 'And I am willing to compromise.'

Somehow she managed to take a step back from him. 'You'll allow me to come to Italy for my holidays, you mean?' she murmured shakily. 'No thank you, Marcus. I'll pass on that.'

'And I wouldn't blame you for passing on that. I don't want to be a part-time parent in the holidays, myself.'

'Then don't leave England.' Her voice held a husky tremor that made it sound more of a plea than an ultimatum.

'I have to.'

'She must be some woman if you are choosing her over your son.'

'I'm not choosing anyone over my son,' he said firmly. 'I'm hoping I can have it all.'

'Nobody can have it all, Marcus,' she said quietly. 'Not even you.'

'When I've made up my mind to something, I usually get what I want.'

The quiet confidence of that last remark made Gemma's heart thud heavily and unevenly in her chest.

'Look, I haven't got time for this,' she murmured. She

glanced beyond him towards the office and noticed that Henry Perkins was looking directly at them. 'I can't afford to slack today. In case it's escaped your notice, things are pretty hectic in here. The managing director is in and there's an important board meeting.'

'Yes, I know.' Marcus glanced at his watch. 'I'm going to have to go.'

'Well, don't let me detain you,' she muttered sardonically.

His dark eyes seemed to sear through her. 'So I'll pick you up tomorrow night, seven-thirty.'

Gemma made no reply. Arguing with Marcus was getting her nowhere. Maybe the best way to deal with this was to allow him to think he'd won and then just phone his secretary tomorrow and cancel.

'Good.' Marcus seemed to take her silence as acquiescence. 'I'll see you later.'

Gemma felt like collapsing in a heap as he turned to leave the room. She felt as wrung out as if she had just been through the spin cycle of her washing machine. But she wasn't going to let him win, she told herself firmly. She would hold her nerve and refuse to meet him tomorrow and hopefully he would realize that if he left the country he would be leaving his son as well.

'By the way.' He turned suddenly and looked at her. 'Now that I've taken over, you can be assured that your application for the position of editor will be treated with fairness and impartiality.'

'Taken over?' She repeated his words in confusion. 'What do you mean, *taken over?*'

But she was alone in the room now and he had closed the door quietly and firmly behind him, leaving her with a slowly dawning sense of horror.

Marcus nearly walked straight into Richard Barry,

who was still hovering outside Gemma's office door, this time minus the coffee, Marcus noticed.

He was younger than Marcus had imagined. In fact, he looked even younger than Gemma…probably about twenty-four or twenty-five. He had an unruly shock of thick blond hair and a worried expression in his grey eyes.

So this was the man who had started trying to play dad to Liam, started to hang around Gemma. Marcus instantly disliked him. He wasn't Gemma's type at all…was he? Despite the dark suit he looked like he'd just escaped from some trendy boy band.

'You're Liam's dad, Marcus Rossini, right?' he said, extending his hand. 'I'm Richard Barry—'

'Features editor, yes. I know who you are.' Marcus shook his hand.

'I've heard about you, too,' Richard said with a grin. 'Liam mentions you quite a bit.'

He had a weak handshake, Marcus noted.

'He's a great little chap, isn't he, I'm very fond of him,' Richard continued brightly when Marcus made no reply.

'Yes, he's quite a character.' Marcus felt like gritting his teeth. 'You can go on into Gemma's office now if you want. We've finished our discussion…for now.'

'Thanks.' The younger man smiled and moved away from him. 'See you around, then.'

'Oh, you can count on it,' Marcus replied with soft emphasis.

CHAPTER THREE

'WHAT on earth is going on?' Richard murmured as he watched Marcus being greeted enthusiastically by the MD, before being steered towards the boardroom.

'I think we have our answer as to who is behind the take-over bid,' Gemma said in a tone that wasn't at all steady. They were both momentarily stunned into silence as the vice president of *Modern Times* arrived in the office and went straight over to shake Marcus's hand.

'And I think we can safely assume it was a successful take-over bid as well,' Richard said, with a low whistle of surprise.

No wonder Henry Perkins looked stressed, Gemma realized bleakly. Once Rossini House had decided to take them over they wouldn't have stood a chance. It was like a plastic toy soldier trying to stand up to an invading army.

'But why would Rossini want *Modern Times*?' Gemma shook her head in disbelief. She could hardly take this in. 'We're hardly in the big league. Why would Marcus Rossini buy us out?' Even as she asked the question she was remembering the look of determination in Marcus's eyes as he told her he usually got what he wanted. And suddenly she had her answer. What he wanted was Liam.

He owned the house she was living in. He owned the company she worked for. It seemed Marcus was taking her over piece by piece, and his ultimate goal was to get Liam.

'Hey, don't look so worried. Marcus seems like a nice enough guy.'

'Looks can be deceiving,' Gemma murmured distractedly.

'I'd say your promotion is in the bag,' Richard said confidently. 'Rossini knows you are over-qualified for the job. In fact, this could really work in your favour. He could offer you something even bigger and better with one of his other imprints. The sky could be the limit—'

'Richard, come back in from dreamland,' Gemma said impatiently. 'I think it's more likely that I can kiss my prospects here goodbye. Marcus won't give me the promotion.'

'How do you know that?'

'Because I know Marcus, and I know what he really wants is Liam, and if I don't hand him over—which I won't—then I'll be out of here.'

'Come on, Gemma. I think you are over-dramatising things. He's not a member of the Mafia, he's a wealthy, upright businessman with a reputation to uphold. He'd hardly take over a company just to get his child. This is big business.'

'This is chicken feed to Marcus Rossini,' Gemma maintained firmly.

'Well, even if you're right and he has bought this place with ulterior motives in mind, it won't get him anywhere. Apart from offering you incentives and pleading with you, there is nothing Marcus Rossini can do to get his son—nothing.'

'You think not?' Gemma looked up at him uncertainly. She really wanted to believe that.

'Honey, he could have all the money in the world but

the judges will still come down on the side of the mother. He must know that.'

Gemma started to feel calmer. 'I suppose you're right...I mean, it's not as if I'm a bad mother, is it?'

Richard smiled and perched on the edge of her desk. 'You are a wonderful mother and Liam adores you.' He reached out and touched her face in a gentle caress. The contact was similar to the way Marcus had traced a finger down and along her skin a few moments ago, but this stirred no feeling of fire inside her, created no chaos, no wild clamour of heartbeats...nothing. Gemma wished it had, and the feeling of emptiness and panic welled up inside her all over again.

'How about I take you out tomorrow night for dinner?' Richard suggested lightly.

'I'm seeing Marcus so we can discuss the future.' She felt the words cause a tremor inside her.

'Okay, well, Saturday night, then. We'll have dinner and take in a movie as well. How's that?'

'Sounds like fun.' Even as she accepted the date, Gemma's thoughts were backtracking towards what she had just said. Without even realizing what she was doing, she had told Richard she was seeing Marcus tomorrow.

Was she really going to go for dinner with Marcus after all her strong and determined words to the contrary?

'Anyway, I'd better get back to my desk, pretend to be busy whilst the new boss is in the building.' Richard smiled.

Gemma smiled back, but she was only half listening.

'And don't worry, Gemma.'

Easy for him to say, Gemma thought darkly as the door closed behind him. Marcus always got what he wanted. Freddie had told her that a long time ago, only he had said it in an admiring way. Freddie had adored his big brother, had hero-worshipped him. Long before Gemma had even met Marcus, she had heard all about him from Freddie.

Even now, when she thought about Francis Rossini— Freddie, as his family and friends affectionately called him—there was still an element of pain.

They had met at Oxford University and an instant friendship had sprung up between them. It was hard not to like Freddie; he was so full of enthusiasm and fun. Wherever Freddie was, there was sure to be a crowd of people gathered around him, laughing and having a good time. He had cut a dashing figure around Oxford in his bright red sports car and women had flocked to him, adoring his dark Latin good looks.

Francis Rossini could have had any woman he wanted but he had wanted Gemma. And that was where the problem had started because, although Gemma had thought Freddie was wonderful, she hadn't been in love with him. From the first moment he had kissed her she had known he wasn't the man for her and she had gently tried to tell him so.

'I love you dearly as a friend,' she had told him firmly. 'But the chemistry between us isn't right.'

'You want thunderbolts and lightning?' Freddie had said, undeterred. 'Then let me take you to bed and I'll give you the best electrical storm you've ever known.'

'No electrical storms, Freddie,' she had said, trying not to smile at the melodramatic tone of his voice. 'Just friends.'

But it had made no difference; Freddie had still pursued her with fervour. He had showered her with flowers and gifts. And in the final year at University, just before they graduated, he had proposed. Gemma had been stunned. She hadn't thought Freddie was that serious! In fact, he had had a bit of a wild reputation where women were concerned and she had assumed that a lot of his displays of affection were just down to his Latin charm. As gently as she could, she had turned him down.

He had taken the refusal well, and they had continued to be friends, but Gemma had been careful to keep him at a distance, never to see him on his own but always to be accompanied by their circle of friends.

After graduation, Gemma had found it difficult to get the kind of job she wanted. She had gone for interview after interview and everywhere the answer had been the same; her qualifications were good but they were looking for someone with more experience.

'How do you get experience if no one will give you a chance!' she exclaimed in disgust on her fourteenth interview of the week. 'I could be the best damn person in the world for this job but you're never going to find out if you don't employ me.'

'We're a national publication group, Ms Hampton,' the editor said patiently. 'We need someone experienced for this position. However, I do have something that might suit. There is a vacancy for a junior on features—'

'I'll take it,' Gemma said instantly.

'Well, I haven't told you yet what it entails.'

'It doesn't matter. I won't be there long, once you discover how good I am.'

The editor smiled at that. 'I like your style, Ms Hampton. Welcome to the *Morning Sentinel*.'

The job was even more menial than she had expected. The pay was lousy, as were the hours, and the main job skills needed seemed to be making tea and being the chief gofer. But she hadn't minded because at least she was in where the action was, and she was content to wait for the chance to prove herself.

That chance came sooner than she had anticipated. The paper wanted to run an article on Marcus Rossini, but the man in control of the Rossini publishing empire guarded his privacy fiercely and never gave interviews. Gemma seized her opportunity and went straight to Freddie to ask for his help.

'If I pull strings and get you an interview, what's it worth?' Freddie asked, a gleam of mischief in his dark eyes.

'I'll treat you to dinner at the Ritz.'

'How about accompanying me to my sister's wedding this summer? I'm short of a date.'

'Freddie, you are never short of a date. You have any number of glamorous woman falling at your feet.'

'But it's not them I want.'

She looked at him in consternation, scared suddenly that he still harboured romantic feelings for her.

Immediately he held up his hands. 'Hey, I'm not getting any ideas. I'm just asking you as a friend. My father's house has enough bedrooms to sleep an entire football team. And everyone would love to meet you. You'll love it…and you'll fall in love with Rome.'

'Rome! The wedding is in Rome!' Gemma's eyes widened. 'I couldn't possibly go with you, Freddie. It's too far away.'

Freddie laughed at that. 'It's a couple of hours on a plane.'

'People will think I'm your girlfriend—'

'Well, you are a girl and you are a friend, aren't you? Anyway, do you want this interview with my big brother or not?'

'That's blackmail, Francis Rossini,' she admonished sternly.

'That's life, Gemma Hampton.' He grinned back.

And so, against her better judgement, she agreed. She was hungry for success and she knew the interview would be a coup, launching her career forward in style. But she hadn't been prepared for it to change her life quite so radically.

Gemma remembered everything about that first meeting with Marcus in vivid detail.

She remembered his office looked more like a penthouse suite than a place of work. Huge chesterfield settees graced one end and picture windows commanded fabulous views out over Green Park.

Marcus was seated behind his desk but he rose to his feet as she walked in. As their eyes met she felt the impact of that glance almost as if he had touched her.

'Good afternoon, Mr Rossini,' she said politely, hoping that she didn't sound as nervous as she felt. There was something awesome about Marcus, something that made her feel suddenly shy and awkward. 'Thank you for agreeing to see me.'

As Gemma's hand was grasped in the firmness of his handshake she felt a jolt of electricity flow through her.

Had her hand lingered too long in his?

Afterwards she wondered a lot about that. The moment had a misty blur of unreality; the only thing she knew was that she was totally captivated. It was as if those thunderbolts that she had joked about had suddenly crashed around her, an electric storm of unimaginable proportions whipping up inside her.

'Pleased to meet you, Ms Hampton,' he said formally.

Gemma noticed that, like his brother, his English was perfect, with hardly a hint of an accent. 'Please call me

Gemma,' she said huskily. And he smiled—a smile that did unimaginable things to her insides.

'Then you must call me Marcus.' He waved her towards the chair opposite his and then sat back down behind the desk again.

'You seem to have made a big impression on my younger brother,' he said easily.

'I wouldn't go that far,' Gemma said with a smile. 'But we are good friends.'

'Just good friends?'

The coolly asked question threw her senses into disarray.

'Yes…just good friends.' She tried to keep her voice light, unsure if he was just making polite conversation or if he was taking a more personal interest. As she looked up into his eyes she found herself hoping sincerely it was the latter.

'Would you mind if I record our interview? It's just so I can check back and make sure I have my facts right.'

'By all means.'

As she took her recorder from her bag Marcus left the office momentarily to say something to his secretary.

'Sorry about that,' he said with a grin as he returned and sat down again. 'Now, fire away with your questions.'

He seemed to be studying her intently and she wished that she had worn something more exciting than her blue suit and that she had put her hair up instead of allowing it to fall freely around her shoulders. She wanted to look as stylish and as beautiful as she was sure the women he dated would look.

She cleared her throat nervously. 'So, Marcus, would

you mind if I asked you about the background of the Rossini publishing house first?'

'By all means.' He settled more comfortably in his chair, almost as if he were about to watch an entertaining film. He seemed very at ease, extremely relaxed, and there was a gleam of amusement in his eyes as if he knew she was nervous.

Honestly, life could be very unfair sometimes, Gemma thought wryly. She had been nervous about the interview to begin with because it was her first really important one. The fact that she found herself over-whelmingly attracted to the man she was interviewing wasn't helping.

He just wasn't at all what she had been expecting.

She had thought he was going to be an older version of Freddie. But, although Freddie was almost as tall as Marcus and their colouring was similar, jet dark hair and eyes that were almost coal black, they were worlds apart in looks. Next to Marcus, Freddie, who was her own age, suddenly seemed terribly young...somehow very immature.

At thirty-three, Marcus Rossini was spectacularly handsome and all male. There was an air of power and sophistication about him and the dark eyes that held hers were cool and serious and seemed to reach into her very soul.

'Your father founded the Rossini publishing business, I believe?' With difficulty she made herself concentrate.

'That's right. I took over the reins six years ago, after my mother died and my father lost interest in the busi-ness.'

'Your mother was English, wasn't she?'

'Yes, she was from Surrey. Freddie has obviously been filling you in on the details.'

'Well, he's told me a few things. You were very young for such an awesome responsibility. Did you find the pressure hard at first?' she pressed on, not wanting to be sidetracked from her line of questions.

Marcus grinned at that. 'I thrive on pressure, and I love a challenge.'

The phone rang and he snapped it up and it was several minutes before Gemma could resume her interview.

The same thing happened just a little while later and after the third and fourth interruptions Gemma started to get irritated. 'Do you think you could get your secretary to hold your calls for a while?'

He looked unrepentant. 'I'm sorry, Gemma, but as I explained to Freddie, I am a very busy man.'

It was then that Gemma took a calculated risk. 'Well, maybe now isn't a good time. Maybe we could continue our discussion in more congenial surroundings later on. How about dinner tonight?'

He fixed her with that quizzical, deep look that she was beginning to recognise. For a second Gemma thought he was going to turn her down and tell her she either put up with the interruptions or she did without the interview. 'Okay, dinner tonight. It's a date,' he said casually. 'But on one condition.'

'Yes?' She felt suddenly breathless.

'You leave your recorder at home.'

'Okay, but I must warn you my shorthand isn't very good,' she said with a smile.

'Well, I promise I'll take things nice and slow,' he drawled lazily.

Something about the way he said that, the way he looked at her, made her senses leap.

'Come to my place for about seven-thirty. That way we can be assured of no interruptions.'

Had she imagined the look in his eye as he said that, Gemma wondered later, as she frantically went through her meagre wardrobe looking for something suitable to wear.

In the end she borrowed a designer outfit belonging to her flat-mate, Jane; a silky, pale grey creation that managed to look sensual and yet smartly chic at the same time.

She felt more nervous than ever as her taxi turned in through gates leading down to a huge Georgian residence that backed out on to the river Thames. There was a feeling inside her that she was out of her depth. She wanted to focus entirely on the interview so that she could write an article that would get her noticed at work...but disturbing her train of thought was the little fact that she was deeply attracted to Marcus Rossini. There was a part of her that was hoping it wouldn't all be business tonight.

A housekeeper opened the door to Gemma and led her through to a drawing room that was furnished with antiques that were stylishly in keeping with the Georgian era. A log fire blazed a welcome in a large open grate. 'Mr Rossini will be with you in a moment,' the housekeeper said, closing the door behind her.

She probably only waited for Marcus for about five minutes but it felt like an eternity. The ornate clock on the sideboard chimed the half hour and Gemma noticed the framed photographs beside it and went over to have a look. She had just lifted one up when Marcus walked in.

'Good evening, Gemma.'

'Evening.' She put the photo down and swung around to face him, feeling slightly breathless as their eyes connected.

'You look very nice.'

'Thank you.'

As Marcus's eyes swept over her admiringly, she sent up a silent thank you to her friend, Jane.

He walked closer to her and she thought he was going to shake her hand but to her surprise he kissed her on each cheek in true Mediterranean style. For a moment she was so close to him that she could feel the warmth of his body radiating against hers. The scent of his aftershave pervaded her senses, clouding her mind, and she felt a rush of desire sharper than anything she had ever known.

As he stepped back and she looked up into the darkness of his eyes she knew beyond a doubt that she really wanted this man…wanted him with a fierceness and a passion beyond even her wildest dreams.

'I see you've been admiring my gallery,' he said, looking at the photos beside them.

'Yes.' Grateful of the excuse to turn her attention away from him, she picked up the photo she had been looking at before. 'Are these your brothers when they were young?'

'Yes. This is Freddie.' He pointed to a cheeky-looking child who was at the front of the picture. 'And that is Leonardo…and next to him Bruno, Nicholas and then me.'

Gemma looked with interest at the photograph of Marcus as a young teenager. Even then he had been good-looking.

'And are these your sisters?' she asked, picking up the photo next to it and studying the two young women, who were dark haired and very beautiful.

'No, I have only one sister.' Marcus pointed to the

young woman to the left of the picture. 'That's Helene. She's getting married in a few months' time.'

Gemma remembered her promise to attend the wedding. 'And who is the girl next to her?' she asked, trying not to think how Freddie was going to feel when he found out she was attracted to his brother.

'That's Sophia Albani. She is a friend of the family— her father and my father were business partners. They started the publishing house together.'

'Really? I didn't realize that Rossini House had started as a partnership.' She was instantly interested in an angle she could use for her article.

'Yes, Filippo Albani was my father's closest friend. They were in business together for quite a while. They went their separate ways in the late seventies when my father bought Albani out.'

'Was it an amicable split?'

Marcus smiled. 'You have your reporter's hat on now, I hear it in your voice.'

'Well, that is why I'm here,' she said lightly.

'Yes.' He reached out and touched her face in a feather-light caress that sent shivers racing down her spine. 'But I hope that isn't the only reason.'

The door opened at that moment. 'Dinner is served Signor Rossini,' the housekeeper announced, her cheerful tones cutting through the sudden tension and excitement curling between them.

Maybe she had imagined it, she told herself over the delicious meal. Maybe Marcus hadn't been making a pass at her, because his manner throughout the meal was, although charming, impeccably polite and correct, with no hint of the dangerous undercurrent of passion.

Somehow she managed to resume her questions over

the meal. Marcus told her in fascinating detail about the business split between his father and the Albani family.

It was a story Gemma itched to write, a story of friendship and big business. All had ended happily, it seemed, and the two men were still good friends today. Filippo had gone into politics and was now a well-known member of the Italian parliament.

'So is the interview finished?' Marcus asked suddenly as he leaned across to fill up her wine glass.

'Just about.' She grinned at him. 'Apart from the personal details, like are you dating anyone special at the moment…any wedding bells on the near horizon?'

'The only wedding on the near horizon is my sister Helene's. What about you, are you seeing anyone special?'

The sudden way he turned the question back on her took her by surprise. 'No, no one serious.'

'Good.'

The way he said that, and the way he looked at her, made her heart miss several beats.

The housekeeper came in to clear the table.

'Maybe we should retire to the other room and make ourselves more comfortable,' Marcus said, pushing his chair back. 'Then maybe I can turn the tables and shine the spotlight on you. You can tell me all about yourself.'

'There's not that much to tell.' She followed him back to the drawing room and sat on the settee, watching as he put another log on the fire.

'I don't believe that for a moment.' He sat in the chair opposite her. As she glanced over and their eyes met she found herself wondering what it would be like to be kissed by him. And the need to find out was like an ache inside.

'It must have been nice growing up as part of a large

family,' she said, trying desperately to turn her mind away from such dangerous ground. Marcus Rossini was out of her league, she told herself firmly. He was almost ten years older; he was a sophisticated and worldly-wise man who probably ate women like her for breakfast, and then promptly forgot about them as the next willing woman fell at his feet.

He nodded. 'We're quite a close family. All of us work in the same business…except for Freddie, of course.' He smiled. 'Freddie has always been a law unto himself. Considering he is the only one of my brothers currently living in London, I hardly see him.'

'He's probably too busy enjoying himself.'

'I know. I keep telling him he'll have to get a job soon, but he pays no attention.'

Gemma smiled and noted the undercurrent of teasing affection in Marcus's voice. He obviously cared a great deal about his brother.

'So, have you got any brothers or sisters?'

Gemma shook her head. 'No, my father died when I was eight and there was just Mum and I.'

'Was that lonely?'

Gemma thought about that for a moment. 'Not really. Mum did a great job bringing me up on her own. But I think it was difficult for her sometimes because she had no family around her at all, no network of support. I used to find myself worrying about her quite a bit because she worked so hard and always looked so tired… Anyway…' She trailed off in embarrassment, wondering why she had told him all that. 'I don't know why I'm telling you this. *I'm* supposed to be interviewing *you*, not the other way around.'

'I was hoping the interview was over…apart from the

personal stuff.' There was a gleam of humour in his eyes.

'Ah, yes, let's get back to that,' Gemma joked and then some spark of mischief made her repeat something his brother had once told her about him. 'Freddie says you have had numerous beautiful women in your life, and that you break hearts.'

'Francis should watch what he says to members of the press,' Marcus said lightly.

'Don't worry, it's off the record.' Gemma grinned. 'In fact, as I have no tape recorder with me, I might have to come back to check I have my facts straight on any of this.'

'I hope you do.' Marcus held her eyes for a long time and she felt her heart speeding up in her chest. Warning bells rang deep inside her, and she found herself finishing her drink hurriedly and standing up. 'Well, I really ought to be going,' she said brightly. 'Thank you for the interview and for dinner.'

'You're welcome.' He also got to his feet.

'I had better ring for a taxi.'

'I suppose so.' As he walked towards her she felt every nerve in her body tighten in anticipation.

He reached out and lifted her chin so that her eyes were forced to hold with his. Then he lowered his head and without warning he kissed her with an intensity and a passion that sent rivers of fire running through her.

'I've been wanting to do that all night,' he said softly as he moved back.

'So have I,' she admitted huskily.

He moved closer and kissed her again. The only sound in the room was the fire burning greedily in the grate and it seemed to echo the heat inside her. Never had she felt this wild intensity of desire. It was incredible…it was terrifying. Because she didn't want to move back; she wanted so much more.

As his hands started to move over her body she welcomed them.

She felt him touch her breast through the silk of her blouse, his thumb caressing her, feeling how she hardened instinctively. Then he kissed her again, his mouth possessing her totally in the most sexual kiss she had ever experienced.

'Ever since you walked into my office this afternoon, I've wanted to do this.' His hands moved beneath her top and pushed the lace of her bra to one side, cupping the warm curves of her body in his hands. The feeling of his skin against her naked flesh made her gasp with need.

Her body was so close to his she could feel the strength of his arousal and she wanted him even closer. His fingers teased her erect nipples, and she longed to be free of the constraints of her clothes, to feel his body against hers, taking total possession.

'God, you're beautiful.' He kissed her neck and the side of her face before finding her lips again in a kiss that was even harder and more demanding, making her body crave his and press even closer.

Then suddenly he pulled back from her, leaving her shaking and torn with desire.

'Why have you stopped? Don't stop.' Her voice was a husky plea, and he smiled.

'Let's go upstairs.' He took hold of her hand and led her towards the door. She went willingly with him, her heart thundering so hard against her chest with wild anticipation that she was sure he could hear it.

He brought her up into an exquisitely lovely bedroom. A four-poster bed dominated the room, draped with white embroidered cotton. A fire blazed in the Adam fireplace. Outside the window there was a view towards the river, just glimpsed through a tracery of trees. It was snowing, and there was a silent tranquillity about the scene that was totally at odds with the raging heat inside Gemma.

Then she noticed the champagne that was chilling on the bedside table and the two champagne glasses.

'It looks like you were expecting me to stay?' Her eyes moved to his.

'Let's say I was hopeful,' he replied with a lazily attractive smile.

The arrogant confidence of the man threw her senses into confusion. And suddenly she was angry. Was he so used to having any woman he wanted that he just took it for granted that he only had to snap his fingers and a woman would come to him? Or maybe he just thought that she was easy?

That thought really unsettled her. The fact was that she was far from 'easy'. She'd had a lot of boyfriends and all of them had tried to get her into bed—all of them had failed. No one had ever turned her on enough for her to want to go the whole way. In fact, she had started to wonder if there was something wrong with her, if maybe she was just not capable of feeling such intense passion. But a few moments ago that fear had been well and truly shattered. At twenty-three she was still a virgin, but it wasn't because she was frigid—it was because she needed the right man to ignite the fire inside her. That that man now thought she was easy was galling in the extreme.

'Hey, don't look so annoyed.' He reached out and touched her face but she flinched away from him before the touch of his fingers could disturb the clarity of her thinking.

'I think I should go, Marcus. I'm sorry…this is just all happening a little too fast.'

'Yes, I suppose it is.' He grinned teasingly. 'But I only promised to take things slowly with the interview, not with what happened afterwards. And I've got a confession to make.'

'Oh, yes?' She watched warily as he opened the champagne and poured it into two glasses. 'What is it?'

'I asked my secretary to keep interrupting us this afternoon so that I could suggest seeing you tonight.'

'You are incredibly sure of yourself, Marcus Rossini.'

'Maybe I am, but I was just about to ask you to have dinner with me when you asked me first.' He grinned and there was a gleam of such charming mischief in those dark sexy eyes that she felt herself smiling back.

'So I did,' she admitted.

'And I have to confess I'm not the most patient of men. It's taken all my self-control to sit through dinner and answer your questions. You're very distracting, you know…extremely desirable, and that top you're wearing skims over your figure in a very tantalizing way.'

'Does it?' She felt her heart start to speed up again. There was something about the way he was speaking, the way his eyes were moving over her, that was mesmerising.

'If wanting someone is a crime, then I'm definitely guilty.' He put the champagne bottle back on ice. 'All evening I've wondered what it would be like to kiss you. Hold you. How you'd taste…how your body would feel against mine.' He glanced back at her.

There was an electricity rippling through Gemma now that made her writhe inside with longing. She had never experienced anything like it in her life. Where other men had struggled to arouse her with caresses and kisses, this man could switch her on like a light bulb with just a few words and the touch of his eyes.

She stood awkwardly in the middle of the room, telling herself that she should turn and leave, but unable to.

'Come here.' Although he held out his hand to her, the words were a command.

'I'm not going to sleep with you, Marcus Rossini, because you are far too arrogant for my liking,' she said sternly, yet at the same time she was crossing over to stand beside him.

'That's perfectly okay with me…' He reached and pulled her down beside him. 'Because I wasn't planning on doing much sleeping.'

Arrogance like that in any other man would have made Gemma turn tail and leave, yet with Marcus the power he exerted over her held a dangerously intoxicating edge.

'Tell me you want me.' He trailed a finger down over her cheek and the feeling sent butterflies fluttering in her stomach. Then he laced his fingers through her hair and held her so that he could kiss her with an expert passion that made her senses reel. 'Tell me,' he demanded huskily as he pulled away again.

Looking deep into his eyes, Gemma could feel herself trembling with need. 'You know I do,' she whispered unsteadily.

She liked the dominant way he started to undress her. The firm, confident way he took her into his arms, the words he murmured against her ear.

Marcus Rossini knew what he was doing when it came to seduction. He was a master at turning a woman on and he found erogenous zones she never knew she had. He turned her from a cool and controlled person into a wanton hussy totally under his spell. She would have done anything for him…anything.

When finally she lay naked and trembling with desire beneath him, she sobbed for him to take full possession of her, unable to take the sweet ecstasy of need any longer. She cried out as he entered her and there was a sharp moment of pain before pleasure took over again.

But he pulled back from her instantly. 'Are you okay?'

The concern in his voice made her insides melt like wax under a flame.

'Yes.' She reached up, running her fingers through the dark, soft texture of his hair. 'Don't stop.' Her words trembled unsteadily and then she reached to kiss his lips with a sweet and yearning passion, pulling him down towards her again. He tempered his passion with gentleness after that, rocking her and cradling her in his arms until the world seemed to turn to liquid around her in a dizzying hue of astonishing and wild sensations.

Afterwards they lay wet and hot in each other's arms and for some reason they both started to laugh. He kissed her on the tip of her nose and smiled down at her. 'Wow…' he murmured huskily.

'You can say that again.' She wound her arms around his shoulders, holding him tight against her, and she had never felt so complete or so happy.

Now just remembering the wildness of that first time and the intensity of pleasure made her heartbeats increase, made her body tingle with a deep, aching void.

She got up angrily from her desk, furious with herself for thinking about such things. Okay, they had enjoyed a wild and tempestuous affair for a few short months. But that was all it had been…an affair. Marcus had never cared about her in any deep, meaningful way; she had just deluded herself into thinking he had. The reality of the situation was that Marcus had just been using her.

Gemma opened the filing cabinet and raked blindly through the contents of the drawer. She needed to concentrate on her work and put memories of Marcus out of her mind, because they didn't help. She found the file she was looking for and sat back down at her desk just as the phone rang.

'Ms Hampton?' a voice at the other end enquired.

'Yes.' She was busy taking notes from the file while she spoke, her mind only half on the call.

'This is Mrs Robertson from the nursery. I'm afraid I'm going to have to ask you to come and pick Liam up. He really isn't at all well. He has a temperature of one hundred and four.'

Suddenly everything that Gemma had thought was important that day melted away. 'I'll be right there,' she said swiftly.

CHAPTER FOUR

THE board meeting finished at the same time as Gemma emerged from her office. She was vaguely aware of Marcus in the centre of a group of men and there seemed to be a lot of backslapping going on and a lot of frivolity, which was a total change from the sombre mood this morning.

Henry Perkins looked over at her in consternation, noticing the handbag over her shoulder and the purposeful glint in her eye as she headed towards the reception area. 'Gemma, are you going somewhere? This isn't a good time to leave the office because I'm just about to call another meeting.'

'I'm really sorry Henry, but my son is ill and I'm going to have to pick him up from nursery.'

Henry frowned.

'What's wrong with him?' It was Marcus who asked the question.

'I don't know. He's got a very high temperature.' As she was speaking Gemma was walking away. She didn't care how busy it was, or how bad a time it was for her to leave—she was going.

She pushed the button on the lift and then spoke to Clare on Reception. 'I doubt I'll be back this afternoon, Clare. So will you put the transcript of the interview with Rick Simmons on Richard's desk. Oh, and don't forget to send Ali for the photos we need.' It was an effort to concentrate on work; she just wanted to be with Liam. One hundred and four was a very high temperature.

The lift doors opened and she stepped in, but before they could close Marcus stepped in with her. 'I'll come with you,' he said. 'I've finished here, anyway.'

'There's no need,' she assured him quickly. The last thing she wanted was Marcus's company. 'I'll phone you on your mobile to tell you how he is. He probably just has a summer cold.'

'If that's the case then I'll pick him up and you can get back to work. You've got a busy day in the office anyway.'

Gemma glanced over at him sharply. 'So you can accuse me of being a bad mother to some judge at a later date?'

'Now you're being ridiculous.'

'Am I?' She stared over at him. 'I know how you operate, Marcus. I've figured you out.'

'Have you?' His eyes held with hers for what seemed like a long moment. 'Then you'll know I was just trying to be helpful.'

'Just trying to take over, you mean,' she muttered under her breath. 'I know what you're up to, Marcus. I know why you've bought *Modern Times*.'

'Do you? And why's that?' he asked calmly.

'Because it puts you in a position of power over me and you are going to use it to exert pressure to get Liam.' She spoke matter-of-factly now. 'But it won't work.'

'I hate to disillusion you but I've bought this magazine because it was a good investment. I'm a businessman first and foremost.'

'Yes, when it suits you,' she grated sarcastically. 'But I don't trust you one inch, Marcus Rossini, and under the circumstances I'd prefer to go and see to Liam myself.' In an effort to end the conversation she smiled at him over-brightly. 'So just go away and leave me alone.'

Far from looking upset or annoyed, Marcus simply looked amused. 'You know, I'd almost forgotten what a fiery temperament you have,' he drawled huskily. 'I always did enjoy sparring with you. You are a very worthy opponent.'

As their eyes held she was suddenly very aware of the close confines of the lift and earlier memories filtered uncomfortably back into her mind. Memories of how fiery things had once been between them. And how that fire had spilt over into the bedroom in a wild and turbulently wonderful way.

The lift doors opened into the basement car park and it was a relief to step out and away from him. Hurriedly, she fumbled in her bag for her car keys.

'We may as well take my car,' Marcus said easily.

Gemma frowned. 'I thought I made myself clear. I'm going over there on my own, Marcus. It doesn't take two of us.' Nervously, she dropped her keys and, before she could retrieve them, he swooped to pick them up for her.

'Thanks.' She held out her hand, but he was walking on in front of her now.

'Yes, well, I'm finished for the day, anyway,' he said over his shoulder.

'Marcus!'

'I'm parked over the other side.' He was striding between the rows of cars so quickly that she practically had to run to keep up.

'Marcus, will you hand me my keys back?'

He ignored her totally and, as they approached his black sedan, he unlocked it with a flick of a button and climbed in.

Hell, but the man was infuriating, she thought angrily. She wrenched open the passenger door and glared at him. 'Marcus, will you hand me back my car keys, please?'

'Get in or I'll leave you behind.' As if to illustrate his point he started the engine.

'For heaven's sake!'

He revved the engine and, alarmed that he really might just go, she hurriedly jumped into the car. 'This is ridiculous. I don't know what you're playing at.'

'I'm not playing at anything.' He reversed the car out of the space and then casually tossed her keys over on to her knee. 'I'm accompanying you over to the nursery. I don't think that's unreasonable.'

Gemma said nothing to that. *She* thought it was unreasonable…but then she was starting to think everything Marcus did was unreasonable. He was so damn arrogant, he thought he could do or say or *have* anything he wanted. Well, he couldn't, and she was going to prove that to him if it was the last thing she did. He might have taken over the company she worked for, but he wasn't taking her over as well.

The car roared smoothly up the ramp and out into the bright mid-afternoon sunlight. She glanced at the clock on his dashboard. It was almost fifteen minutes now since the nursery had called.

She hoped Liam was okay, and that he wasn't crying or distressed. He had looked flushed this morning. A curl of guilt stirred inside her as she remembered that. Maybe she shouldn't have sent him to school? But she had honestly thought he was hot because he'd been running around playing.

'I thought Liam was a bit off-colour on Sunday,' Marcus remarked nonchalantly into the silence as he turned the car into the heavy flow of traffic.

'Did you?' She frowned. 'You never said anything.'

'That's because I didn't see you when I dropped him back…as per usual,' he added dryly. 'But I did mention it to Joanne. She said he was probably overtired.'

'Well, Mum was possibly right. You let him stay up far too late when he stays over.'

'Do I?' Marcus glanced over at her wryly.

'Yes, you do. He's always exhausted when he comes back from your house. You try to pack far too much into a weekend—he's only four.'

'I don't pack too much in. We have fun together, that's all.' Marcus's voice was derisory. 'But maybe you've forgotten what that word entails.'

'I beg your pardon?' She glared at him furiously. 'What the hell do you mean by that?'

'Well, you are always working, aren't you? The fact is, Gemma, that you are a very ambitious career woman, you always have been.'

'Your point being?' she asked crisply.

'The point being that you have a four-year-old, and I know how tough your job is, how much pressure must be on you, especially now you're working so hard towards the promotion you want. Balancing that and Liam can't be easy on your own. There can't be much time left over for just having fun with him.'

'We have lots of fun and I'm managing very well.' Her voice was stiff with fury. 'And if this is your way of trying to tell me I'd be happier without him, then you can just forget it. My world revolves around Liam. I adore him.'

'I know you do.'

'And, as for having fun, in case you've forgotten, I let you have the relaxing time with him at the weekends. I cope with the routine stuff in the middle—the important things like making sure he eats sensibly and has brushed his teeth. Real life isn't letting him eat sweets at midnight and every meal at hamburger joints.'

'I don't let him eat sweets at midnight.'

'Hah!' Gemma turned away from him to stare sightlessly through the car window. 'That's not what he tells me.'

'I don't care what he tells you.'

'And we do have fun together. I took him for a picnic on Saturday when you let him down—'

'I didn't let him down. I just had some business to deal with which made it impossible to have him on Saturday morning.'

'Well, whatever.' She shrugged airily. 'But it's funny how it's okay for you to have business pressures and not me.'

'I didn't say that.'

'Didn't you? Sounded like it to me. And, for your information, I not only work hard, I play hard, Marcus,' she added icily.

There was a long moment of silence between them as she strove to get her temper back under control.

Marcus glanced over at her. He noted the tense way she was sitting. The way her black skirt had ridden up a little on her long shapely legs.

'In fact, Richard and I are planning to take Liam away on holiday to Spain soon…not that it's any of your business.' She turned to look at him again, her eyes glinting like chips of blue ice.

'Really?'

'Yes, really,' she said coolly. This wasn't entirely true. Richard had mentioned going away together but she hadn't given him an answer yet. She was still unsure about how involved she wanted their relationship to get. However, telling Marcus this half-truth did give her a momentary feeling of pleasure, especially as she noted how his hands tightened slightly on the steering wheel. 'And Liam adores Richard,' she added for good measure.

'Well, I'm pleased for you, Gemma, but I have to admit I'm surprised that you and Richard are hitting it off so well.'

'Why's that?' She was momentarily distracted from her anger by that statement.

'He just doesn't strike me as your type.' He grinned over at her. 'You're spirited, ardently passionate, very tempestuous... Richard strikes me as being a bit dull for you, and a trifle weak—not the type to be able to handle you at all. And certainly not the type to turn you on.'

'That is total rubbish!' His statement horrified Gemma, but the thing that most dismayed her was that he was absolutely right. Richard didn't turn her on. She did find him a little dull. Immediately the thought crossed her mind she was cross with herself. Richard was one of the nicest men she had met in a long time. And anyway maybe safe was better than exciting...look where exciting had got her, she thought as she glanced over at Marcus.

She had once delighted in the dominant hold Marcus had held over her senses. Sexually speaking, she had found his strength of character and his confident manner a complete turn-on. He'd only had to look at her in a certain way and say a few words, and she had been his. Richard didn't have that effect on her at all...in fact, no other man ever had. But there was no way on earth she would ever let Marcus know that. He was bigheaded enough.

'I absolutely adore Richard,' she lied vehemently. 'He

really turns me on *and* he's a gentleman,' she added for good measure.

'Unlike me, you mean,' Marcus grinned.

'Yes, unlike you.'

'Well, I may not have been a gentleman but I definitely turned you on.'

'Go to hell, Marcus.'

He laughed at the outrage in her tone. 'You really don't like being reminded of what we had, do you? Why is that?'

'Because it's something I've forgotten long ago,' she said heatedly.

'You know what, Gemma? I don't believe you,' he said quietly. 'For one thing, you never forget your first time…' He watched her face flare with bright red colour.

'I rest my case,' she said tersely. 'You are no gentleman.'

He pulled into a parking space outside the nursery. 'And, just for the record, I absolutely loathe and detest you,' she added, reaching for the door handle and getting out of the car.

She had hoped that he would wait for her in the car, but he followed her inside the building. They walked side by side, not speaking, and the atmosphere between them was thick with tension.

Good, she thought heatedly. She hoped she had really hurt him, because he was insufferable and impossible.

As they turned the corner of the corridor, she saw Liam sitting beside Fiona Campbell, the young woman who had been his nursery teacher for the last year. Gemma felt a jolt of shock as she looked at her son. His eyes were large and feverish and seemed to dominate his tiny face, and his skin was a strange greenish-white colour. As he saw her he started to cry and she ran towards him to take him in her arms.

'It's okay, darling. It's okay, Mummy is here.' She held him tight against her. 'How long has he been like this?' she asked his teacher quietly as their eyes connected over the child's head.

'He's been worse over the last ten minutes,' she answered softly. 'He's complaining of a severe headache...' She paused before adding gently, 'And I've noticed a rash.'

The word *meningitis* instantly jumped into Gemma's mind, and the thrust of fear that shot through her was unbelievably sharp. She looked over at Marcus, her eyes wide.

He came and crouched down beside the child. 'Liam, let me see you,' he said gently, holding out his hands. The calmness of his voice stilled the child's cries and he obediently turned.

'Now then, what's all this noise?' Marcus held a hand over his son's forehead to check his temperature. His manner was quiet and assertive and it seemed to soothe Liam's distress...and Gemma had to admit it soothed her too. She was suddenly fiercely glad that he was there.

'Okay, let's look at this rash.' He checked Liam's arms and legs and then pulled up the blue T-shirt to check the child's stomach. The rash was only faintly visible, but it was there.

'We'll have to get him to a doctor immediately,' Gemma said, trying to soften the urgency of her tone so as not to alarm Liam.

'Yes, I think you are right.' Marcus reached to pick the child up.

'Thanks for looking after him, Fiona,' Gemma said hurriedly.

The woman nodded and smiled sympathetically. 'Hope he feels better soon.'

'I'll keep you posted.'

'Bye, Liam, hope you feel better soon.' Fiona waved at him but he was clutching hold of Marcus and his cries were getting louder and more distressed.

Gemma practically had to run to keep up with Marcus as they headed for the car, but this time she wasn't complaining. She sat in the back seat with Liam on her knee while Marcus drove. The traffic was horrendously heavy and the short drive to the nearest hospital seemed to take an eternity. Liam was so hot she could feel his body burning against hers. And between cries of pain and distress, he seemed to be slipping in and out of consciousness.

'It's okay, darling, we are nearly there.' She kept stroking his forehead, trying to soothe and reassure him.

'My head hurts,' he whimpered.

'It'll be okay. We'll soon get a nice doctor to make it better,' she whispered, kissing him and holding him tight.

Marcus watched her from time to time in the rearview mirror, noting the tenderness in her touch and the way Liam clung to her. 'Is he still as hot?' he asked.

'Yes…he seems to be burning up.' Her eyes connected with his in the driving mirror and for a moment there was a unity between them, a shared feeling of anxiety that went deeper than any words.

Marcus pulled the car through the gates to the hospital and then parked directly at the front of the accident and emergency department. He hurried around to help Gemma from the back seat, taking Liam up into his arms. Then together they ran through the front doors.

In one way it was a blessed relief having doctors and

nurses taking over and yet in another the sense of help-lessness as she watched the medical staff around him was the worst feeling in the world. She tried to concentrate on the questions the doctors were asking her. What was his name? How old was he? What was his medical history? What had he eaten that morning? And all the while his cries tore into her and she just wanted to go over and pull the nurses away, take him into her arms again and just hold him.

'Mrs Rossini?' The doctor pulled her attention away from Liam again. 'Has he been vomiting?'

She shook her head. At the back of her mind she registered the fact that the doctor was calling her Mrs Rossini. It was an easy mistake, as Liam's surname was Rossini.

'How long has he had the high temperature?'

She faltered a little before answering. 'He was hot this morning but I didn't think he had a temperature. He'd been running around playing…' She trailed off as guilt struck her forcibly. 'I shouldn't have sent him to school, I should have stayed at home with him today…'

'He can't have been that bad this morning.' Marcus reached and took hold of her hand, squeezing it reassuringly. 'His teacher didn't ring until after two o'clock this afternoon, remember.'

She nodded and bit down on her lip. She felt as if she was holding on to control by a whisper. She wanted to cry like Liam, uncontrollably and noisily. She felt the weight of her tears pressing down in her throat like a golf ball wedged solidly there. 'Has he got meningitis?' she asked, her voice a half whisper of fear.

'Too early to tell what it is yet. We're going to run a few tests.' The doctor sounded very matter-of-fact. 'Don't worry, Mrs Rossini, he's in good hands.'

The medical staff allowed them to remain present as they carried out their tests and they both tried to soothe and placate Liam so that he would allow them to proceed. It was one of the most traumatic and difficult afternoons of Gemma's life and she had never felt more helpless or more scared. There was also an overwhelming sense of relief at having Marcus by her side. He was incredibly calm and his strength helped her to stay focused and to hide her fear from Liam. She noticed how wonderful he was with his son, how he could cajole and soothe and even raise a smile under the most stressful of circumstances. No wonder Liam loved him so much, she thought, her heart thumping unsteadily against her chest as she watched them together. It had always been obvious from the way Liam talked about his dad, the way his eyes lit up at the mere mention of Marcus's name, that there was a close bond between father and son. But Gemma had never witnessed the relationship so closely before and it was so special and so touching that it took her completely aback.

They put Liam in a small private room with the blinds pulled firmly across to keep the evening sun out. He was quieter now, drifting in and out of consciousness. Gemma and Marcus sat beside him, taking it in turns to bathe him with cool water to help keep his temperature down.

Liam looked tiny in the big bed, so vulnerable and so ill that Gemma's heart ached.

'He'll be okay,' Marcus said gently as he noted the look of anguish on her face when two of the doctors who had been treating him stopped outside the door to consult their notes.

She nodded. She had to believe that, it was all that was getting her through. 'I wish I could change places with him,' she whispered huskily. 'I wish it was me who was so ill.'

Marcus reached out and took hold of her hand. It was the second time that day that he had done that and she found it strangely comforting. 'Thanks,' she whispered.

'Thanks for what?'

'For being here…for being so good with Liam.'

'He's my son, Gemma. You don't need to thank me for that.' His voice was gruff, but his hand didn't leave hers. She stared down at it and her eyes blurred for a second with tears. She was very glad that the room was in semi-darkness. 'I'm sorry I said some of those things to you today,' she muttered unsteadily.

'Which things in particular?' He sounded amused for a second.

'Well…you know…that I loathe and detest you. You're not really that bad…'

'Hey, don't go too far with the compliments,' Marcus said with a half-smile. 'You'll only regret it once Liam is up and running around again.'

'Probably.' She smiled through the haze of tears and looked up at him. 'You are just so damn irritating and arrogant sometimes.'

'Hey, you're spoiling things now.'

She smiled. 'But you're a very good dad,' she admitted huskily. 'Sometimes the fact that he adores you so much really winds me up. I hear about you a million times a day.'

'Well, I hear about you a trillion times a day,' Marcus said with a small smile. 'Mummy always kisses him better when he falls down… Mummy has a special way of making soldiers for his boiled eggs… In fact, everything you do is wonderful, according to Liam.'

'Really?' Her voice trembled a little.

'Yes, really.' He reached out and wiped a tear away from her face with a gentle finger. 'He loves you to bits.'

'I've been thinking a little about what you were saying to me earlier—how I work so many hours. Maybe you're right. He's going to big school soon and I haven't had as much time as I'd have liked with him as a baby.'

'You're doing fine, Gemma,' he said softly. 'It's not easy being a single parent.'

She shrugged awkwardly. 'But maybe I shouldn't have been so awkward and so proud…maybe I should have accepted more help from you.'

'It's not too late,' Marcus said quietly. 'We can start again.'

Suddenly Gemma wanted to go into his arms. She wanted him to hold her close and reassure her that there was going to be a chance of starting again. 'You think he'll be all right, don't you?' she asked softly.

'Yes, I do. I think he'll be fine.' He said the words firmly, as if he wasn't going to allow Liam to be ill, as if he had it all under control.

But as they looked over at the child who seemed so peaceful now in his hospital bed, they both knew that this was beyond their control.

The door opened and the doctor came in. Gemma knew from the look on his face that he had the test results.

They both stood up and Marcus put a steadying arm around her waist.

'Well, the good news is that your son does not have meningitis,' the doctor said immediately, and Gemma felt herself go weak with relief.

'But he is giving us cause for concern. He appears to have a rare viral infection that is working its way through his immune system.'

CHAPTER FIVE

'I DON'T know, Mum, that's all they've said.' Gemma
stood out in the corridor at the pay phone, one hand over
her ear so she could hear what her mother was saying
amidst the noise around her. 'They can't give him an-
tibiotics because it's a viral infection. We just have to
wait now for his fever to break. They say once they've
got his temperature down he'll have turned the corner.'

Gemma glanced down the long corridor and saw a
nurse going into Liam's room. 'I'll have to go, Mum. I
don't want to be away from him for too long…yes,
Marcus is here, thank God.' Her voice shook slightly.
'I'll ring you as soon as there is any change.'

She put the phone down and hurried back. It was nine
in the evening now and through the window she noticed
the sun was still blazing outside. Entering Liam's room
felt like entering a bad dream, the blinds were drawn
and he lay surrounded by monitors, still deeply uncon-
scious. Marcus and the nurse were talking quietly.

'Any change?' Gemma asked, anxiously looking from
one to the other.

'No, no change,' the nurse said gently. 'I was just
telling your husband that there is a canteen up on the
third floor. Maybe you should take it in turns to go up
and have something to eat, Mrs Rossini. It could be a
very long night for you and you need to keep your
strength up.'

She supposed she should correct the assumption that
Marcus was her husband, but it seemed easier just to let

it pass. 'Thank you, I'll have something later,' Gemma murmured. The last thing she wanted right now was food. She went over to check on Liam, stroking his hair back from his forehead.

The nurse went out of the room, leaving them alone, and Marcus came to stand at the other side of the bed. 'What did your mum say?'

'She wanted to come down. But I told her there was no point. I tried to play it down a bit so that she wouldn't worry too much.'

Marcus nodded. 'You should sit down.' He indicated the chair behind her. 'You look exhausted.'

'Do I? I feel okay.'

'Well, sit down anyway. I'll get us both a coffee from the machine outside.'

'Aren't you going to go up and have something to eat?'

'Like you, I suspect, I couldn't face anything right now.'

She nodded and pulled the chair behind her closer towards the bed. In the few moments that Marcus was gone there was just the steady bleep of the monitor and she felt her anxiety levels rise even further. 'Please get better, Liam,' she whispered to him. 'Get better and Mummy will give you anything you want.'

He lay so still that he almost looked unreal, with not a flutter of his eyelashes or a hint of any movement.

Marcus returned with the coffees. He handed hers over and then sat down at the opposite side of the bed. She noticed he'd taken his jacket off and his tie, and the top couple of buttons on his white shirt were unfastened. Even in this time of anguish she couldn't help but notice how attractive he was. There was a slight shadow at his jawline and his dark thick hair looked ruffled, as if he had been running his hand distractedly through it. For a second Gemma longed to be closer to him, to be able to lean over and straighten the collar of his shirt, to brush the stray strand of hair on his forehead back soothingly. She wanted to touch him so badly it hurt.

He looked over and caught her eye and immediately she felt foolish.

'I can't remember the last time we sat and had a coffee together,' he said softly.

'No….neither can I.' She looked away from him towards Liam. She noticed how much he looked like his father, same texture of hair, same dark colouring.

The sad thing was, she could remember exactly the last time they had sat and had a coffee together. It had been a few weeks before his sister's wedding, the day she had tried to tell him she was pregnant.

'When Liam is up and about again we'll go out for dinner together.'

'To discuss your move to Italy?' She looked back at him, her heart thumping against her chest.

'To discuss where we go from here.'

'Don't go back to Italy, Marcus. Please.' She hadn't intended to say those words but they came out in a sudden rush. 'Liam needs you.' There was a part of her that wanted to add that she needed him too, but she stopped herself. She was feeling vulnerable because Liam was ill. She didn't need Marcus Rossini, she told herself crossly. She had managed perfectly well without him so far, why should she need him now? 'And don't tell me that you are taking him to Italy with you, because that's just nonsense. He needs us both, Marcus.'

'I agree. But I have to go back,' he said quietly.

'Why?'

'Because the business there needs me.'

'So this has nothing to do with you getting married?'

She watched one dark eyebrow lift in surprise.

'Liam told me,' she said flatly. 'He overheard you on the phone the other night.'

Marcus went very quiet for a moment. 'He must have heard my conversation with my father.'

'So it is true, then?'

'Well, I haven't actually proposed yet,' Marcus said dryly. 'Give me a chance to get around to it before the jungle drums start declaring it to the world.'

'I'm not writing an article on you now, Marcus,' she said softly. 'I'm just asking because of Liam.' She glanced away from him over at her son.

'Well, put it this way. If there is any news on the wedding front you'll be the first to know.'

'Thanks.' She didn't look back at him and she didn't ask if he was finally going to settle down with Sophia. There was no way she would allow him to think she was jealous—his accusation about that this morning still rankled. And anyway he was right; it really was none of her business.

'Do you think Liam's colour is a little better?' she asked, putting a hand on the child's forehead.

'Maybe. Does he feel any cooler?'

She shook her head. Then her eyes moved to the monitor beside her. The steady beep seemed to reflect the beating of her heart.

'I don't know if he can hear us or not, but a few moments ago I promised him anything he wants if he'll just get better.'

'That could cost you very dear,' Marcus said with a half-smile.

'I'd do anything if I could just have him back.'

'Would you come to Italy with me?'

The quietly asked question made her heart miss a beat and she looked across at him in shock.

'Why are you asking me that?' Her voice was so low as to be almost a whisper.

'Why do you think?' His mouth twisted ruefully. 'If this has taught us anything, Gemma, it's taught us that Liam needs us both. I watched how you held him on your knee today in the back seat of my car, how he clung to you, how you kissed and cuddled him and made him feel secure, and the knowledge of how much he needs you hit me like a force ten gale.'

Gemma didn't say anything to that, but she knew exactly where he was coming from because the same feeling had hit her as she had watched him with Liam a little while later.

'If you came to Italy we could be a family together. Think how much that would mean to Liam.'

How could they ever be a family when he was marrying someone else? Maybe he thought they could all be friends together…she had a sudden vision of being invited to the wedding, of wishing him and Sophia all the best for the future. She knew for Liam's sake that would be a good thing but she didn't think she would be strong enough to be able to do it. The very idea made her feel slightly sick inside.

'I don't know, Marcus…my life is in England. Things here are just starting to go in the right direction for me.'

'Richard might be the right direction for you, but is he right for Liam?'

She hadn't been thinking about Richard. She had been thinking about the fact that she liked her job, about her mother and her friends. She was settled in London. Asking her to give that up to live on the sidelines of his life was asking a lot...even if, deep down, she knew it would make her son happy.

'I don't know, Marcus, I can't think about this now.' Distraught, she looked back at Liam.

Please wake up, darling, she thought fiercely. Please.

As she stared at him, willing him to recover, she thought she saw the flicker of his eyelashes. 'Liam?'

Marcus stood up and rang the button for the nurse to come.

'Liam?' Gemma stroked his hair. 'Liam, darling, wake up.'

To her immense relief his eyes suddenly opened and locked with hers. 'Mummy, where am I?' he asked, his voice small and frightened.

'You're in hospital, remember?' Gemma swallowed down a lump in her throat. 'The doctors and nurses are making you better.'

'Can I go home now?' Liam looked over at his dad.

'Not just yet.' Marcus leaned closer and stroked a hand tenderly and protectively down over Liam's face. 'You've given your mum and me a bit of a scare. How are you feeling now?'

'I'm okay.'

The door opened and the nurse came in. She smiled as she saw Liam was awake. 'Looks like our patient is on the mend,' she said brightly.

'I think his temperature is coming down,' Marcus said, moving away from the bedside to allow the nurse to check him over.

'Yes, you're right.' The nurse smiled at Gemma. 'The doctor will be along in a few moments to check him out but it looks like the worst is over.'

The relief that swept through Gemma as she heard those words made her feel weak inside. And as Marcus put an arm around her shoulder she turned and buried her head against his chest, allowing herself to draw strength from his closeness for just a moment.

She was unprepared for the fierce stirring of emotion that the close contact with Marcus had on her senses. The last time she had been held like this in the circle of his arms they had been lovers, and although that had been years ago the familiar feelings that surged through her now made it feel like yesterday. In that instant she remembered everything about their relationship, not just the heat, passion, and fiery intensity, but the tenderness and depth of feeling. She had loved him deeply, wildly…completely. His betrayal had hurt so much that she had thought she would never get over him. And maybe she never had. Maybe there was a part of her that would always love Marcus.

That thought was so horrifying that it made her break contact with him and move swiftly away.

As the nurse left Liam's bedside she went to sit beside him.

'Can we go home now?' Liam asked her tentatively. 'I want to play with my train set.'

'You must be feeling better.' She smiled at him through a haze of tears.

'Why are you crying, Mummy?' He looked at her in consternation.

'Because I'm happy and I'm relieved.'

As soon as the doctor confirmed that Liam was getting better Gemma went out to phone her mother again. When she returned to the room Liam no longer had the monitors attached to him and the nurse was tucking the blankets in around him, telling him he should settle down to sleep.

'Dr Tompkins said they'll be keeping him in for a

couple of days' observation but he thinks that all being well he'll be able to go home on Sunday,' Marcus told her quietly as she stood back giving the nurse room to work.

'Well, that's good news.' Gemma couldn't bring herself to look at Marcus; the memory of the way she had clung to him a few moments ago was too fresh in her mind. She was appalled at herself for such weakness.

'If you want to go home and get some rest I'll stay here with him,' he continued briskly.

She shook her head. 'Thanks, but I really don't want to leave him.'

As soon as the nurse left the room Gemma moved to sit next to the bed again. 'How are you feeling now, darling?' she asked gently as Liam looked over at her.

He smiled. 'Okay…a bit sleepy.'

She brushed his hair back from his forehead with a tender hand. 'So close your eyes and rest,' she said softly.

For a while he seemed to fight against sleep but his eyes were heavy and soon his breathing deepened as he drifted into a peaceful sleep.

Marcus left the room and she wondered if he was heading home, but he returned almost immediately with a blanket and a pillow in his hand.

'You may as well make yourself as comfortable as possible in that chair,' he said gently, handing them over to her.

'Thanks.' Gemma was finding his thoughtfulness and his gentleness over these last few hours very hard to handle. She didn't want him to be nice to her; it made it harder to remember the reasons why she had to keep her distance from him.

'You don't have to stay,' she said quickly as he sat back down in the chair opposite.

'Yes, I do, Gemma,' he said quietly. 'I don't just want to be around Liam because he's my responsibility. I love him too, you know.'

'Yes, I know you do.' For a moment their eyes met and then she looked quickly away from him again and busied herself arranging the pillow behind her head. 'Well, I suppose we should try and get a few hours' sleep,' she said brightly.

But trying to sleep in the chair was almost impossible. Not only was it extremely uncomfortable but her mind was in turmoil. She kept running through the events of the day. They flashed through her mind like a series of picture cards in a wildly jumbled order.

Liam looking so ill, Marcus holding her hand, the tests and the uncertainty. Then Marcus asking her to go to Italy with him. Had he meant that, she wondered, or was it just something he'd said in the heat of the moment?

Then she remembered the feelings that had flooded through her when she had been held in his arms and that made her even more restless. She had to keep in mind that, although Marcus was marvellous with Liam, he was still the man who had hurt her badly. He was not a man to fantasize about, she told herself fiercely.

Her mind flashed back to the moment when they had sat having coffee together. She had lied to him when she had casually agreed that she couldn't remember the last time they had done that. Of course she remembered...it was etched in her mind for all time.

She'd persuaded him to meet her in her lunch hour at a coffee bar around the corner from her office and he had agreed with a hint of reluctance. 'I've got a really hectic day ahead of me, Gemma.'

'So have I,' she had told him swiftly. 'But let's just grab a quick lunch together. I need to talk to you.'

Gemma had arrived at the coffee bar first and had found a table at the back of the shop. She remembered the place had been packed with people from surrounding offices and shops, and the din of voices and the noise of the steam machine they used for espressos and cappuccinos had made her wonder nervously if this was the right place to tell Marcus the momentous news that she was pregnant. But she had tried to tell him when they were alone, and the problem was that as soon as they were behind closed doors Marcus would reach for her and everything else would be forgotten.

Their affair had been going on for over three months, and it had been the most exciting three months of Gemma's life. She had felt as if she were on some wild and wonderful roller-coaster ride. Their time together in the bedroom had been wild, tempestuous and utterly blissful. And even out of the bedroom, just hearing his voice had made her body tingle with exhilaration. But their relationship hadn't been at all conventional; outside the bedroom they had talked mostly about work. Gemma had been keen to get ahead in her career and, to her delight Marcus had taken an interest in her professional development.

The interview with him had got her the promotion she had so greatly craved. But Marcus had read her article and told her she could have done better. The remark had hurt, but when he had gone on to tell her where she had gone wrong she had taken note. He wasn't one of the biggest names in publishing for no reason; Marcus had an instinctive feel for good journalism. Not only had he years of experience but it just seemed to run in his veins. So when he had taken her under his wing she had been only too thrilled to have him as a mentor. It had certainly made for sparkling and animated conversations... sometimes too animated; things could get very heated when they disagreed. But for the most part she had taken his judgements and his advice on board and her work had improved. She'd been offered another promotion, but Marcus had thought she shouldn't take it. Instead, he had set up an interview for her with one of his own publications, a paper with a bigger turnover and a prestigious image.

At the time, when she had sat for the interview, it had seemed like the most nerve-racking and important moment of her life. But just over a week later, as she had sat in a coffee shop waiting for Marcus to arrive, all her priorities had changed. And she had realized how little the job really meant to her.

She had discovered a few days earlier that she was pregnant, and the knowledge had gone round and round in her head, blocking out everything else. And she'd been scared because, despite the fierce passion of their union, she hadn't really known what Marcus felt about her. He had never spoken one word of love to her...not one. Oh, sometimes he had murmured words in Italian to her as he held her close and possessed her fully. But they had been just meaningless compliments: he had called her beautiful, desirable...things he could have said to any woman he took to his bed. They had meant nothing.

Those facts hadn't really worried her too deeply until the moment she sat in that café and tried to prepare the words she needed to say to him. And suddenly she had realized how much she wanted him to tell her he loved her—how deeply and emotionally vulnerable she was where he was concerned. The thought of losing him had made her blood run like ice-water in her body: She was wild about him, she adored him, she wanted his baby and she wanted him so much it had hurt.

He had walked into the café fifteen minutes late, his mobile phone to his ear as he had sauntered through the crowds of people. She'd raised her hand to attract his attention and he had acknowledged her with a nod as he sat down in the seat opposite. Marcus had been speaking in rapid Italian but she had followed most of what he had been saying; she had a quick ear for languages and since meeting Freddie and then Marcus her Italian had become almost fluent. It had been a business call, and basically he had been bawling someone out for failing to do what he had asked. It had quickly become apparent to Gemma that he wasn't in the best of moods and she had felt her nerves clench even tighter.

'Sorry about that,' he said to her almost absently as he hung up. 'I've had a hell of a morning.'

'Have you? Mine hasn't been too marvellous either.'

Marcus heard the nervousness in her tone and he smiled in an arrogantly amused way. 'Well, I know why you're so keen to see me this afternoon.'

'Do you?' She was totally taken aback, wondering if he'd guessed her secret. How could he know she was pregnant? She'd only recently found out herself.

'I suppose the anticipation is driving you wild.' He grinned.

She frowned in confusion. 'Marcus, I don't—'

'It's okay. I suppose my telling you is a bit unorthodox but you'd be hearing through the regular channels soon, anyway. You've got the job. Ben Hardwick loved you.'

'Oh, I see.' The job she'd applied for was the last thing on her mind but she managed a smile.

'So congratulations are in order. They will probably want you to start in about eight weeks' time, so there's no rush giving in your notice at the *Morning Sentinel*. I'd wait a couple of weeks.' Marcus held up his hand to attract the attention of the waiter and she noticed that despite the rush hour crowd he came over to Marcus immediately.

That was the thing about Marcus: he had that air of power, that ability to make everyone rush to do his bidding straight away.

'You didn't pull strings for me to get the job, did you, Marcus?' she asked, momentarily distracted from what she really wanted to talk about.

'Well I pulled enough strings to get you the interview. But you did the rest yourself. You're a damn good journalist, Gemma, and Ben recognised that.'

Marcus never gave praise lightly and the words pleased her.

The waiter arrived with their coffee and Marcus glanced at his watch. 'I'm afraid I'm not going to have time for anything to eat, Gemma. I've got to get back to the office. I've got loads on because I'm having to take some days off soon to go to Rome for Helene's wedding.'

It struck her at that point that Marcus had not asked her to accompany him to his sister's wedding. It seemed an ominous sign. Maybe he knew that Freddie had already invited her? 'I've been meaning to talk to you about that,' she said casually. 'You know, don't you, that Freddie has asked me to accompany him to your sister's wedding?'

Marcus paused with the cup of espresso coffee half-way to his lips. 'No, I didn't know.'

'I thought that was why you hadn't invited me yourself.' She waited for him to offer some excuse for not doing so. But none was forthcoming. He just looked at her, a cool expression in his eyes.

'I haven't seen Freddie for a while. Obviously, you have.'

'Well, I see him occasionally. He asked me to go with him to Helene's wedding ages ago. Before I met you, in fact.' She was suddenly at pains to explain in case he jumped to the wrong conclusion and thought there was something going on between her and his brother. But she needn't have bothered; Marcus wasn't the jealous type and he wasn't the slightest bit interested or concerned. He glanced at his watch. 'I'm really going to have to go, Gemma. I've got an important meeting this afternoon. So, if there is nothing else you want to discuss…?'

She wanted so much to tell him she was pregnant, had built herself up for it all morning, but she couldn't just blurt it out when he was being so cool and businesslike. 'There was one other thing,' she managed to say quietly. 'But I suppose it can wait.'

'Good. I'll phone you and we'll arrange to go out for dinner soon, okay?' He reached to kiss her, but the kiss was absently brisk. '*Ciao*, Gemma.'

She watched him walk away from her with a sick feeling inside. Not only had she not told him she was pregnant, but she had a horrible feeling that huge cracks were appearing in their relationship.

That feeling more than intensified over the next two weeks because he hardly had time to speak to her on the phone, never mind see her.

She sat next to Freddie on the plane to go to Rome. She had never felt more confused or alone in her life. It seemed that Marcus had just dropped her out of his life for no real reason.

Gemma wanted to confide in Freddie but, as she had never discussed her relationship with his brother in the first place, she didn't know where to begin. So she told herself that she'd find a quiet time during the weekend to speak to Marcus, either at his father's house or some time during the wedding and that they'd sort things out. But that chance never presented itself and the first time she saw Marcus was when they got to the church. She glanced across and noticed the very glamorous brunette seated next to him.

'Who is that?' she asked Freddie curiously.

He glanced across too and smiled. 'That's Sophia Albani, the woman Marcus is going to marry.'

The matter-of-fact words hit Gemma like a freight train.

'I didn't know Marcus was engaged,' she said icily.

'Well, it's not official yet, but it has always been understood that they will marry one day. They were childhood sweethearts. They are just waiting until Marcus's spell of running the English side of the business is over before setting the wedding date. Sophia doesn't want to live in London, you see—she absolutely hates the place. Although I think she might be getting ready to compromise and go to England because the separation is killing them both. They miss each other like crazy.' Freddie lowered his voice to a whisper. 'In fact, I had a very embarrassing experience this morning. I went around to Marcus's house to deliver the flowers for the buttonholes and there they were in the front lounge *in flagrante delicto*. Those two can't keep their hands off each other.' He noticed the sudden pallor of Gemma's skin and smiled. 'Hey, don't look so shocked. Some people do have sex before they get married, you know, and my brother is a very red-blooded male. In fact, I don't know how he's managing to survive the distance without Sophia.'

'Maybe he has another woman in London.' Gemma's voice was brittle.

'Probably.' Freddie laughed. 'A bit on the side, as you British like to say, and why not? He's still single, he may as well enjoy himself and have a few flings while he still can.'

The words rang in Gemma's ears like instruments of torture. And suddenly everything became crystal clear. She had her answer as to why Marcus hadn't invited her to his sister's wedding, why he had never uttered any words of love. Why he had backed away from her over the last couple of weeks. He didn't love her; theirs had just been a very steamy and brief affair, nothing more. And he was probably livid that she was at his sister's wedding, worried in case Sophia would find out about them. The knowledge hurt like crazy.

She didn't know how she managed to get through that day. Every time she looked around she saw Marcus and Sophia, and it was an unbearable torture. Sophia looked so happy, so much in love as she looked up at him, and Gemma felt humiliated and used.

When she finally found herself alone with Marcus for a few minutes during the evening celebrations, she didn't know if she wanted to cry or to smack his face.

'You forgot to tell me about your childhood sweetheart when I interviewed you for my article,' she said derisively.

'Well, maybe you should have done further background research, Gemma,' he replied coldly. 'I know I certainly should have done some on you. Maybe that way I wouldn't have been so surprised by the fact that you were attending my sister's wedding with Freddie. And we could both have saved ourselves some discomfiture today.'

'Feeling a little awkward, are you?' His cool audacity took her breath away. Obviously, he was only bothered about Sophia finding out about them, not about how badly he had behaved. He hadn't even tried to make excuses.

'Well, aren't you?'

'Why should I feel awkward? Frankly, I couldn't care less,' she lied coldly, pride coming ferociously to her defence. 'It's not as if we were ever serious about each other, is it? We just had a fling.'

He didn't try to argue with her, just nodded his head grimly. 'Look, Gemma as you seem to be so…' he hesitated before saying dryly, '…*close* to my brother I don't think we should fall out. We had a good time while it lasted,' he said firmly. 'And you've got the job you wanted with Rossini House, so no hard feelings.'

It took a tremendous amount of willpower to remain cool. And she was so glad when Freddie came to her rescue, walking over and placing a proprietorial arm around her waist as he asked her to dance with him.

'I'd love to dance with you, Freddie,' she said, smiling up at him. And she walked away from Marcus without a backward glance. If there was a prize for acting ability that night she would certainly have got one. She danced every dance with Freddie, gazing up into his eyes, ignoring the fact that somewhere across the room Marcus was with Sophia.

She told herself that her heart wasn't breaking, that she didn't care. But inside she felt as if she wanted to die.

Marcus congratulating her on her job with a Rossini publication had been the final insult. Had he seen the fact that he had helped her career as a kind of payment in kind for services rendered? The idea appalled her.

In fact, the first thing she did on her return home was to turn down the job with Rossini House. She didn't want anything that was remotely connected with Marcus.

But she did want her baby. She wanted Liam with all her heart.

Freddie was remarkably supportive to her in the days after they returned from Rome and a new closeness developed between them. But Gemma still didn't tell him of her relationship with Marcus or the fact that she was expecting his baby. Somehow she didn't want to spoil Freddie's glowing image of his brother. He looked up to Marcus so much. It was only when Freddie started to make romantic overtures to her again that she had to tell him the truth.

She could still remember the shock in his eyes when she told him that she was pregnant, that it was Marcus's baby. Even now she felt the weight of guilt. She had shaken Freddie's belief in his beloved brother to the core. And he was incredibly angry. Vowed to go over to Marcus to sort him out.

She tried to calm him down, begged him not to say anything to Marcus because he didn't know about the baby and nor did she want him to. But Freddie wasn't in any mood to listen and he left her apartment in a tearing rage.

Gemma was so worried about him that she rang Marcus for the first time since returning from Rome. He wasn't in and she left a garbled message on his answering machine, telling him his brother was very upset and was on the way over.

But Freddie never arrived. His sports car had spun out of control and left the road somewhere between Gemma's apartment and Marcus's house. Freddie had died instantly.

Even now, five years down the line, thinking about Freddie made Gemma's heart turn over with grief. The police had estimated that he had been driving over a hundred miles an hour and that the accident was entirely his own fault. But, deep down, Gemma didn't agree. She felt responsible because he had been so upset when he left her apartment. Every minute of every day she still regretted telling Freddie about Marcus that night…indirectly, she still felt that the accident had been her fault.

She had said as much to Marcus when he came around to see her a few days later. She had blurted out the truth, that she was pregnant with his child, that Freddie had been furious with him and had been going over to confront him.

Marcus had said nothing. He had looked drawn and ill and had walked away without even acknowledging what she had said in any way. A few days later he had come back and asked her to marry him.

He might as well have put the words, 'It's my duty,' before the proposal itself. There had been no pretence at feelings he didn't possess. Gemma had turned him down just as coldly. 'We don't love each other,' she had said. 'So what's the point? I suggest you go away and marry your childhood sweetheart. At least that way one of us will be happy.'

But Marcus hadn't married Sophia. Gemma guessed that it had taken the other woman all this time to forgive his infidelity. It was one thing forgiving an affair, quite another when a child was involved. Especially as that child always took centre stage in Marcus's life.

But obviously Sophia had come to terms with that now. She arrived from time to time to see Marcus in London and Liam didn't dislike her.

Gemma thumped the pillow on her chair and desperately tried to rid her mind of the past.

Taking Liam to live in Italy wasn't an option, she thought angrily. As much as she wanted her son to be happy, she could never happily accept Marcus and Sophia living as man and wife on her doorstep.

CHAPTER SIX

THERE was a strange noise coming from somewhere. It sounded like the rattling of china being stacked in a dishwasher. Gemma opened her eyes feeling disoriented. For a second she didn't know where she was. Then she saw the hospital bed and it all came flooding back to her. She sat up, wincing in pain from the cramped position she had slept in, and checked on Liam. He was still fast asleep, but his colour was a lot better. He looked back to normal.

'Bon giorno,' Marcus said gently.

Gemma glanced across at him. Despite also having spent the night in a chair, he looked remarkably fresh and attractive. The dark stubble of his jawline seemed to add a certain edge to his Latin good looks, gave him a kind of sensual come-back-to-bed look.

'Did you sleep okay?' he asked.

'Well, I think I drifted off for about an hour.' Gemma wrenched her eyes away from his. He looked like a male model and she felt a total mess. Her hair had escaped from its ponytail and her black business suit was creased. She ran a smoothing hand down over her skirt. 'Did you sleep?'

'No, not really.'

The clatter of noise in the corridor intensified and she glanced out and noticed they were bringing down the breakfast trolleys.

'Is your neck bothering you?' he asked and she realized she had been rubbing at it absently.

'Yes, I think I was resting at an awkward angle.'

'You were. The pillow dropped and you looked very uncomfortable. I was going to pick it up and try and slide it under your head again but I was concerned that it would wake you up.'

The knowledge that he had been watching her while she slept made her feel self-conscious.

'You were talking in your sleep as well.'

'Was I?' She glanced over at him, horrified by that. As she had been reflecting a lot about him and about the past last night, she hated to think what she might have been inadvertently revealing. 'What did I say?'

'Not a lot that made sense.' He grinned at her. 'Don't look so worried. Your secrets are safe with me.'

'Well, that's a relief.' She matched his teasing tone. 'I'd hate you to find out what I really think about you.'

'It might go to my head, you mean?'

'Something like that.' She moved closer to the bed to look at Liam as he stirred. 'Hello, darling.' She smiled at him as his eyelashes flickered open. 'How are you feeling now?'

Liam yawned sleepily and turned velvety dark eyes on her. 'Okay. A bit thirsty.'

There was a jug of water by the bed and Marcus moved to pour him a glass. 'They are bringing down the breakfast trolleys. How do you fancy something to eat?' he asked, helping the little boy to sit up.

'I don't know.' Liam shrugged. 'Will they have pancakes like you make at home, Daddy?'

'They might do. We'll ask.'

Gemma looked over at Marcus in surprise. 'I didn't know you could cook.'

Marcus grinned. 'I'm obviously better at keeping secrets than you are.'

'Daddy's good at cooking. He can make boiled eggs too, and snake and chips.'

'Snake and chips?' Gemma smiled at Marcus as she fixed the pillows behind Liam so he could lean back. 'That sounds…interesting.'

'Certainly is. You haven't lived until you've tasted my snake…with chips.'

'You burnt it one time, didn't you, daddy, and there was smoke in the kitchen and the smoke alarm was ringing.'

'Okay, son, a little too much information is coming forth now,' Marcus said with a laugh.

Gemma smiled over at him. 'Do you burn snakes in your kitchen often?'

'Only on Friday nights with a nice bottle of Chianti.' Marcus glanced over at her, a gleam in his eye. 'You'll have to come over one night.'

She smiled but didn't answer.

Marcus watched her as she stroked Liam's hair back with a tender hand, noted the watchful concern in her eye as he closed his eyes for a moment. 'Are you still tired, Liam?'

'Just a little.'

'You're bound to be a bit tired,' Marcus said soothingly. 'You were very ill yesterday. It will take you a little while resting to get over it.'

Liam nodded.

The nurse came in and smiled as she saw Liam sitting up. 'Our patient looks much better today,' she said cheerfully.

'He says he is still a little bit tired,' Gemma told her and she nodded.

'How about some breakfast, Liam?' she asked him.

'That should give you more energy, get you further on the road to recovery.'

'Have you got any pancakes?' Liam asked.

The nurse shook her head regretfully. 'No, but we can order you some for tomorrow morning. I've got some scrambled eggs and toast.'

'That would be great, wouldn't it, Liam?' Marcus said positively and the little boy nodded in agreement.

Gemma was surprised at the ease with which he acquiesced; she usually had a major struggle to get him to eat scrambled eggs.

What was more, he ate most of the small plateful of food without having to be prompted.

As they were clearing away the dishes Gemma's mother arrived. 'Well, you look better than I expected,' she said, reaching to give her grandson a hug. 'You had me very worried.'

'I had to have an injection but I didn't cry, Nana,' Liam said.

'Well that's a brave boy.' She sat down on a chair that Marcus brought forward for her. 'Who would have thought when I brought you to the nursery yesterday, Liam, that you would end up in hospital?' she said with a shake of her head. 'I kept thinking about it all night. You didn't look ill yesterday at all. Maybe a bit hot, but you'd been running around.'

'It was certainly a shock when we arrived at the nursery,' Gemma said quietly.

Joanne nodded and looked over at her daughter. 'You look tired. Why don't you let Marcus take you home for a couple of hours' rest and I'll stay and keep Liam company? No point us all being here.'

'No, I'm fine, Mum. I don't want to leave him yet—'

'Your mother is right, Gemma.' Marcus cut across her

The Reader Service™ — Here's how it works:

If offer card is missing write to: The Reader Service, PO Box 236, Croydon, CR9 3RU

NO STAMP NEEDED!

THE READER SERVICE™
FREE BOOK OFFER
FREEPOST CN81
CROYDON
CR9 3WZ

NO STAMP
NECESSARY
IF POSTED IN
THE U.K. OR N.I.

firmly. 'You should take the opportunity while Joanne's here to go home. Not only do you need the break but we should pick up some things for Liam, some pyjamas and his toothbrush.'

Marcus was right. She glanced over at Liam, torn about leaving him, but knowing it made sense to go while her mother was there. 'Will you be okay if Daddy takes me home for a little while?' she asked him and he nodded.

'Will you bring my storybook back?' he asked. 'You know, the one with the dinosaurs in?'

'I will.' She went over to kiss him and give him a hug. 'I'll see you in a little while.'

Marcus gave him a kiss and ruffled his hair. 'Look after Nana,' he said with a teasing grin. 'No wild parties while we're gone.'

Liam giggled.

'Do you think he's okay?' Gemma asked as they left the hospital. 'He does look very tired and yet he slept all night.'

'It's to be expected, Gemma. The best thing for him now is to get as much sleep as possible, allow his body to repair itself.'

They walked out into the fresh morning air. The sky glowed pearly-pink with the promise of a hot day to come and the air was a balmy relief after the stuffiness of the hospital. She breathed in deeply.

'It makes you realize how much we take health for granted, coming out of there, doesn't it?' she murmured to Marcus as he unlocked his car and she got in.

'It certainly makes you get priorities in order,' he agreed with a nod.

They didn't speak for a while as he negotiated the Friday rush-hour traffic going into the city centre.

There was something very calm about Marcus, she thought, watching the way he handled the car. There had been many times over the years when she had been infuriated by that cool and powerful self-assurance of his, yet in a real crisis she had found herself relying on those same qualities, grateful for his strength and his level-headedness. And he was wonderful with Liam…

'I meant it, you know, when I said I wanted both you and Liam to come to Italy with me.' Marcus glanced over at her as he pulled the car to a standstill outside her house.

'I can't think about that now, Marcus,' she said. 'I know you aren't a person who likes to take things slowly. But that is a hell of a big decision and we need to take things one step at a time now.'

'On the contrary. I think we have wasted enough time and we need to get our act together fast.'

'This isn't something we can rush, Marcus. For one thing, neither of us is thinking very clearly at the moment.'

His eyes moved over her face, lingering on the softness of her lips in a way that made her heart stand still. 'On the contrary, my thoughts are crystal clear,' he murmured huskily.

She swallowed hard, wondering nervously if she had imagined the look in his eyes, the sudden flare of sensual tension that had ignited from nowhere.

'Come on, we'll discuss this inside,' he said, reaching for the door-handle.

'I'm really tired, Marcus, and I don't want to argue with you right now.'

'Who said anything about arguing? I think we've done enough of that. We should have a sensible discussion. I'll make the coffee. How's that?'

She smiled. 'What, no pancakes?'

'I'll impress you with my cooking skills at a later date.' His eyes moved to her lips again. 'You have a truly beautiful smile, Gemma, do you know that?' Marcus spoke in Italian, and the sudden compliment and the tone made her blush. It also made her remember the more intimate moments of their time together in the past, times when he had taken her into his arms to murmur private words of seduction against her ear.

'Don't try to charm your way around me, Marcus, because it won't work.' Automatically she answered him in Italian, her heart thumping against her chest so loudly she felt sure he would be able to hear it in the close confines of the car.

'You remember your Italian?' He smiled.

'Of course I remember.' She looked away from him awkwardly, as a sudden vision reared in her mind of them lying naked in each other's arms, him teaching her new risqué phrases and laughing at her blushes.

'That's good.' From the husky satisfaction in his tone she wondered if he had been remembering those moments too.

'Liam speaks Italian when he comes home from your house. That's why I'm still reasonably fluent.' She strove to clarify the point.

Marcus smiled. 'Of course,' he murmured. 'Come on, I'll make that coffee.' He turned away from her and got out of the car.

Part of her wanted to tell him forcefully that she didn't want him coming inside the house with her, yet perversely, as she glanced over at him, there was a stronger part of her that was glad he wasn't rushing off. She was scared of the fact that he could get around her so easily. It smacked of the way he had been able to arouse her emotions so easily in the past. She remembered times when he'd only had to make a phone call to her at work telling her in that arrogant, and yet oh, so sensual tone that he wanted her, and she had felt herself going weak inside with need and desire...

She slotted her key into the front door with a slightly trembling hand. Those days had gone for ever, she told herself fiercely. There was no way that Marcus could turn her on so easily now. She had no need to be afraid of his power over her senses now that she had learnt her lesson.

Gemma led him into the hallway, lifting the post as she walked in. 'I should ring the office and tell them I won't be in today,' she said, forcing her mind to practicalities.

'I'll do it for you,' Marcus said, and then grinned. 'After all, they can't argue with the boss now, can they?'

She didn't know whether to be irritated or amused by that remark. 'You love power, don't you, Marcus,' she said, walking away from him with a shake of her head. 'It's a powerful aphrodisiac where you are concerned.'

'I can think of better aphrodisiacs,' he murmured with a grin as he picked up the phone.

She decided it was better to ignore that remark and went through to the kitchen to flick on the kettle before going upstairs to find some night things for Liam. The sight of his train set curving out from his bedroom into the landing made her heart lurch painfully. She remembered how much he'd been enjoying playing yesterday...and how irritated she had been because he had almost made her late for work. It seemed like weeks ago instead of twenty-four hours.

His bed was still unmade and she went to straighten it. As she picked up his favourite teddy bear from the floor on the way past, she had a sudden terrifying vision of what might have been…if the fever hadn't broken last night… She sat down on his bed, burying her head in her hands for a moment in silent thankfulness.

'Are you okay?' Marcus's voice from the landing made her jump.

'Yes.' She looked up at him and he noticed how blue her eyes were in the pallor of her skin. There were times when Gemma looked incredibly vulnerable. Despite her success in her career and her confident manner, underneath it all he sometimes glimpsed a 'little girl lost' look about her. It was a look that brought out a fiercely protective surge inside him. Made him want to take her into his arms and hold her close.

'He'll be okay you know.'

'I know…it was just such a shock.'

Marcus nodded and looked away from her. Forcing himself not to go over to her, he glanced around the small bedroom, noting the mobiles on the ceiling and the shelves of books. He had to play this very carefully, he told himself. He had made up his mind that he wanted Gemma and Liam back into the centre of his life and he wasn't going to give up, despite the fact that the truce between them was tentative and uncertain. When she had instinctively turned to him last night, allowing him to hold her for a moment in his arms, he had felt they had turned a corner. But she could just as easily turn away from him again and he wasn't going to risk that.

He was going to have to play this with cool determination, using every trick, every strategy at his disposal. Marcus was resolute in his intent. When he left for Italy he would be taking his son and Gemma along with him.

Gemma noticed the way Marcus was looking around

the room with a look of intense seriousness on his face. She realized this was the first time Marcus had been into Liam's bedroom. In fact, he had only ever set foot into the front hallway of this house, and that was on rare occasions when he'd arrived much earlier than expected to pick Liam up.

'Is Liam's bedroom at your place like this?' she asked him curiously.

'Similar.' He grinned at her. 'But it's a bit tidier. I still have Mrs Philips looking after things.'

She remembered his housekeeper well from the times she had spent at his house in the past, and smiled. 'I take it she is as efficient as ever?'

'Oh yes, not a speck of dust would dare to settle around Mrs Philips. I might have to take her with me to Italy as well.'

'Maybe it would just be a lot easier not to go,' Gemma said quietly.

'We've been through this, Gemma. I have to go.' His eyes met hers seriously. 'Nicholas is arriving next week to take over the running of the London office. I fly to Rome the week after.'

Gemma felt a jolt of shock that he was going so soon.

Silence fell between them for a moment as she struggled to come to terms with the news. What the hell was she going to tell Liam? she wondered suddenly. He was going to be devastated.

'It's strange that you gave Liam this bedroom.' Marcus changed the subject. 'It's the one I pictured him in. I used to sleep in here sometimes when I was a child.'

'Really?' She frowned.

He nodded. 'This was my mother's house. We used to stay here when we visited her family in the summer holidays.'

She remembered the letting agent telling her that, only of course she hadn't realized then that he was talking about Marcus. 'I didn't realize,' she murmured. 'And when you told me you owned this house I assumed you'd bought it after we'd moved in.'

'No. I steered you towards viewing it by giving your mother the paper with the advertisement ringed for your attention. I told her I'd already viewed it and it looked like a suitable property. But not to mention that the suggestion came from me. I knew if you found out I was in any way connected to the house you'd stubbornly refuse even to consider it.'

The words fell bluntly between them. She couldn't argue with that because she knew he was right. Her mother had obviously realized he was right as well, because she hadn't mentioned the fact that this house had been Marcus's suggestion.

'In a strange kind of way I've found it reassuring over the years being able to picture Liam's surroundings so clearly, knowing that he was in a good environment.'

'I wouldn't have chosen somewhere that wasn't a good environment for him,' she said quickly.

'I know that. But I'm talking about the atmosphere more than anything—this house has happy memories for me. I've liked the security of knowing Liam is here.'

'And now you want to take him away.'

'To something even better. He'll like my villa. It's in the countryside just outside Rome. There's space for him to play, a large orchard, a stable where he can learn to ride…dogs and cats, and lots of family in the area. In fact, everything to make up a secure and wonderful childhood.'

'You've got it all figured out, haven't you?' She glared up at him, her voice filled with sarcasm. 'And where do I fit into this rosy picture? Are you thinking of shoving me into one of the sheds at the bottom of your orchard where I can conveniently pop out to see Liam when it suits you?'

He grinned at that. 'Not quite.'

Gemma put the teddy bear she was holding down and stood up from the bed. 'I can't come to Italy with you, Marcus. The whole idea is absurd. My life is here.'

'You told me once that Liam is your life.' He watched as she made Liam's bed and then moved towards a chest of drawers to get a pair of his pyjamas out.

'Well, he is…of course.' She hesitated. 'But there are other factors to take into consideration.'

'That promotion at *Modern Times* that you want so badly is mere chicken-feed compared to what I can offer you in Rome.'

Her hand stilled and she looked over at him questioningly.

'There's a position becoming vacant soon for editor in chief at *Élan*.'

Her eyes widened. *Élan* was one of Rossini's flagship publications, a prestigious glossy magazine with a huge European circulation. *Modern Times* was a provincial hick by comparison.

'I thought that would get your attention.' Marcus smiled.

'Meaning?'

'Meaning you always were driven by your career.' His voice was dry. 'It's what brought you to me in the first place, isn't it?'

'I suppose you could say that.' She closed the drawer.

'Oh, come on, Gemma, we both know the main reason you graced my bed for so long was that I was helping to further your career.'

She blanched at those words, too shocked to be able to refute them for a moment.

'I didn't mind that.' He shrugged nonchalantly. 'I didn't want anything serious, anyway.'

'I'm sure you didn't, with sweet little Sophia waiting in the wings for you at home in Italy.' Gemma's voice trembled precariously. 'Don't go all pious on me, Marcus. Because I remember very clearly what happened. And if you remember rightly, I didn't take your job at Rossini back then,' she added sharply. 'And I don't intend to take it now.'

'You didn't take the job back then because you were pregnant and Freddie was going ballistic.'

'It had nothing to do with Freddie.'

The shrill ring of the phone cut the atmosphere between them and she hurried out and over into her bedroom to answer it, scared in case it was the hospital ringing to say there was a change in Liam's condition.

It was Richard and she gave a sigh of relief.

'I just got into the office,' he said. 'And they told me about Liam being in hospital. How is he?'

'He's a lot better than he was yesterday.' Gemma glanced over as Marcus came to stand in the open doorway. 'It's okay, it's only Richard,' she told him, covering the mouthpiece for a moment. 'Why don't you go now? I'm going to take a quick shower and I'll head back to the hospital in a taxi.'

'We haven't finished our conversation.'

'I think we have.' She ignored him and went back to talking to Richard, hoping Marcus would take the hint and leave.

'They said they will be keeping him in for a few more days for observation. Yes, I'm sure he would love you to come and see him. Maybe you should wait until tomorrow, though. Ward C.' Gemma glanced over at the doorway and was relieved to find Marcus had gone. 'Okay, Richard... Yes I'll look forward to seeing you... Bye.' She put the phone down.

The house seemed very quiet, ominously so. She felt her heart beating against her chest as she remembered Marcus's hurtful remarks about her only sleeping with him to further her career! Maybe that was his way of justifying the way he had behaved? She remembered that at his sister's wedding he had made a similar remark to her— 'You've got the job you wanted with Rossini House, so no hard feelings.'

Gemma was fiercely glad that she had turned that job down. She had found life difficult as a single parent working full-time, but at least she had proved that she could stand on her own two feet. She had worked her way up without any help from anyone.

And she wouldn't accept this job offer at *Élan* either, she told herself fiercely. She would do as she had planned and apply for the top job at *Modern Times*. Marcus could go to hell. She had always sworn she wouldn't be under any obligation to him and now she could remember quite clearly why not.

Getting up from the bed, she headed for her en-suite bathroom and quickly stripped off to stand under the forceful jet of the shower. But as her temper faded, the question of how she was going to tell Liam that his father was leaving returned.

Gemma had been a bit older when she had lost her own father; she remembered clearly the devastation she had felt. And she knew how much Liam loved Marcus. He hero-worshipped him.

Stepping out of the shower, she dried herself with brisk angry movements, then wrapped herself in a soft white towel and quickly blow-dried her long hair. It wasn't as if Marcus had died, she tried to reason with herself. Liam would see him during the holidays. That would have to be enough.

Returning to the bedroom to get dressed, she was surprised to see Marcus sitting on the side of the bed waiting for her.

'I thought you'd gone!' She clutched the towel more tightly around her body.

'No. I told you we hadn't finished our conversation.' His eyes swept slowly and deliberately over the long length of her shapely legs. There was something blatantly sensual about the leisurely perusal. It reminded her of the way he used to look at her and disconcertingly she felt her body respond just the way it used to, with a quickening of her pulse-rate and a flare of red-hot excitement.

'I want you to go, Marcus. I need to get dressed.'

'Go ahead,' he said calmly.

Irritated beyond words, she went over to her wardrobe, intending to get her clothes and return to the privacy of the bathroom.

'You asked me where you would live if you came back to Italy,' he said, watching her as she flicked through the rails of clothing.

'It isn't going to happen, Marcus,' she said flatly, clutching hold of the bath-sheet and trying to focus on the clothes in front of her.

'I want you to live with me…as my wife.'

For a second she thought she had misheard him. She turned to look at him, incredulity in her eyes. 'I beg your pardon?'

He smiled. 'You heard me—I want us to get married. It's the only way forward. It's the best thing for Liam… for us.'

The arrogance of that statement made her laugh. 'Now I know you are joking.'

'Here's the deal,' he said, getting up from the bed and walking slowly towards her. 'You marry me and live with me at my villa in Rome and I give you a two-year contract at *Élan*.'

She moistened her lips nervously. 'We don't love each other, Marcus, and there's no way—'

'Think very carefully before you refuse me, Gemma.' The warning in his voice made her heart slam against her chest. 'You assume it's a foregone conclusion you'll get custody of Liam if this goes to court, but nothing is certain in a courtroom. And I'll fight you every inch of the way. Both of us could end up as losers. Do you want to risk that?'

She couldn't answer him. Her breathing felt tight and restricted.

'This way we all end up as winners. Liam has the security of being in a family unit. You get the job of your dreams. I get to keep my son with me.'

When she still didn't answer he continued smoothly, 'I'm a very wealthy man, Gemma. I can offer you a very good lifestyle with everything you want. I suggest we give this our best shot…for Liam's sake. But if you are not happy by the end of your contract with *Élan*, I'll let you go with a handsome divorce settlement. No hard feelings.'

'And in the meantime I live at one end of your villa, like a bird in a gilded cage, and you live at the other? We have a marriage in name only?'

He smiled at that. 'That's definitely not what I'm saying…' He reached up and trailed a hand down over her face in a gentle caress that made her heart race. 'I said we should give the marriage our best shot…'

'You mean sleep together?' Her heart was beating very erratically now.

'Don't sound so appalled. That was the one thing we did very well together in the past…as I recall.'

'Your arrogance never fails to astound me.' She shook her head.

'And the way you are able to lie to yourself never fails to astound me,' he replied silkily. 'Sex was always red-hot between us and you know it.'

'I know nothing of the kind.' She angled her chin up defiantly, her blue eyes blazing into his. 'In fact, I can't even remember what sex was like between us,' she lied vehemently, determined to cut his conceited remarks dead. 'So it can't have been that special. And I wouldn't want you to touch me if you were the last man left on the planet.'

'Really?' His lips twisted coolly.

'Yes, really.'

'Are you angling for a reminder, Gemma…a little taste of how things used to be?' He stepped closer and suddenly alarm bells were ringing loudly inside her body.

'Marcus, I—'

But whatever she had been going to say was cut short by the pressure of his lips against hers. She tried to twist her head away from him, but he held her still with remarkable ease, one hand holding her while his lips carried out a thoroughly gentle yet devastating assault on her senses. For a little while she managed not to respond. Her hands were clenched into tight fists at her side and her lips didn't move beneath his.

His skin was rough and scratchy against hers but for some reason that only served to heighten the sensation of complete arousal inside her. She wanted to respond…she wanted him with a melting weakness that tore into the deepest, darkest recesses of her soul.

His lips knew exactly the way to turn her on. They moved gently at first and then with more heated insistence, dominating her senses until her mind swam hazily with desire and she could do nothing but reach upwards and stand on tip-toe to meet the fierce insistent passion with equal need.

His body pressed closer and his lips moved from hers to trail a heated path to her neck and then upwards to her ear. 'You see, Gemma…you've always been mine for the taking,' he whispered fiercely in Italian.

The arrogant words should have restored her senses, should have made her try to push him away again, but as his hands moved beneath the towel, finding the heat of her naked flesh, her body responded urgently to him.

He caressed the soft curves of her breast, feeling the way her nipples swelled and hardened beneath the gentle encouragement of his fingertips.

'Tell me you want me,' he whispered huskily against her ear.

She was aware that the bath-sheet was slipping down; she could feel the soft material of his suit against her skin, and with it the heat and strength of his arousal.

Little shivers of ecstasy shuddered through her body as his hand slid down over her narrow waist, then lower over the curve of her buttocks before moving to stroke between her legs. She gasped as his hand made contact with the most intimate core of her.

He kissed her neck and the side of her face. 'Say it,' he insisted. 'Admit that I turn you on, that you want me.'

Gemma was almost incoherent with need. The force of her desire was like being held in the grip of a tornado.

She'd never known anything so powerful. She wanted to feel him inside her. She wanted the sweet relief of being as close to him as she could possibly get.

'I want you, Marcus…' The words were almost choked out of her. He moved and kissed her lips again, fiercely this time. His hands left her body to cup her face, holding her still while he ravaged her lips with a sweet searing hunger.

Then, just as she thought she was going to go out of her mind with wanting more, with needing him to possess her body fully, he stepped back.

Dazed, she just managed to catch the bath towel before it slipped to the floor. She held it in front of her with shaking hands, looking up into the darkness of his eyes with perplexity.

'Remember now?' he asked her softly.

She couldn't answer him; she was too dazed…too shocked by the fact that he had actually stopped.

'You see, Gemma. Sexually speaking, I think we'll be fine. Think about it. I'll need your answer by the end of the week.'

Then he calmly turned and left the room, leaving her weak and shaken, wanting him so much it was almost a physical pain.

CHAPTER SEVEN

LIAM made steady progress and by the following day Gemma was told that the doctor would discharge him when he made his rounds of the ward later that afternoon.

'Thank heavens for that!' Gemma's mother was in the room with her daughter and she smiled over at Liam. 'You'll be home by tea-time with a bit of luck.'

'Will I be coming back to your house or Daddy's house?' Liam asked, looking over at his mother.

'You'll be coming back to our house, darling.' Gemma frowned. 'Why are you asking that?'

'Because it's Saturday and I usually stay at Daddy's house on Saturday.'

'Oh! Well, not this Saturday,' Gemma said softly, wondering if this was a disappointment to Liam. Did he prefer staying at his dad's house? she wondered suddenly. The thought was cold in the pit of her stomach.

'Where is Marcus?' Joanne asked, cutting into her thoughts.

'He left in the early hours of the morning. Said he'd be back around eleven.'

Gemma could hardly bear to think about Marcus. The atmosphere between them since the incident in her bedroom yesterday had been so tense it was almost tangible. She was furious with herself for allowing him to touch her and for wanting him so much, furious with him for being so damn arrogant and so sexually adept at turning her on.

When they had met up at Liam's bedside again yesterday, the memory of what had transpired between them had been so disturbing she had hardly been able to look at him. But Marcus had acted as if nothing had happened, chatting about nothing in particular, laughing with Liam and the nurses. The more nonchalant he had seemed, the more the episode took on a feeling almost of unreality. Yet her body had reminded her forcefully that it had been no dream. Her skin had still tingled from the touch of his hands, and she could still feel the imprint of his lips, so dominant, so sensually arousing against the softness of her mouth. Every time she thought about what had happened she felt a fierce thrust of desire that refused to go away, no matter how hard she tried to dismiss it.

'How are you and Marcus getting on?' her mother asked suddenly, and she felt herself blush to the roots of her hair.

'We're getting along okay.' She shrugged and looked away.

'I just wondered how it was going...with you spending so much time together.'

Gemma was very glad when the nurse came into the room, taking the focus of attention away from her. 'You know, I think I had better go and ring Richard,' she said suddenly. 'He said he might come and see Liam this afternoon, and I don't want him to have a wasted trip.'

It was a relief to get out of the room away from her mother's perceptive gaze. But she was only halfway down the corridor towards the phone when Joanne caught up with her. 'So what's really going on?' she asked firmly.

'Mum, nothing is going on.'

'Come on, Gemma, I'm not stupid. There was a

strange atmosphere between you and Marcus yesterday and it wasn't just down to the fact that you were both worried sick about Liam. And today you've been really distracted, and yet Liam's better. The doctors are ready to let him go home.'

'Mum, it's nothing.' She turned, and met the shrewd look in her mother's blue eyes and let her breath out in a sigh. Maybe it would be good to talk about this to someone. Maybe once she had voiced the dilemma, it would help her see things more clearly. 'Okay...but I don't want you to get the wrong idea.' She took hold of her mother's arm and led her over to the side of the corridor by the coffee machine. 'Marcus has asked me to go to Italy with him...as his wife.'

She watched her mother's eyes widen and then a smile of pure pleasure crossed her face.

'I told you not to get the wrong idea!' she said quickly. 'This doesn't mean what you think it means.'

'No?' Her mother shook her head, a smug gleam in her eyes now. 'So what does it mean?'

'It means that Marcus is so desperate to get his son that he's prepared to do anything to get him. He doesn't love me, he just sees me as a necessary part of the equation to get his child—'

'Oh, honestly, Gemma, for an intelligent woman you don't half talk some rot sometimes,' her mother cut across her briskly. 'The reason Marcus has asked you to marry him is that he loves you. It's obvious to anyone with eyes in their head.'

'I might have known you'd start to get all romantic and dreamy about this, Mum.' Gemma shook her head. 'You've always had a blind spot where Marcus is concerned. But the truth is that Marcus views me in a cool clear light. We are compatible...in some ways...' She tried not to blush as she said those words. 'But for the most part he views me as a necessary accessory if he is to have his son in his life. His real love is Sophia Albani.'

'So why isn't he asking her to marry him?'

'I don't know…' Gemma shrugged, at a loss now. 'I really thought he was poised to do just that.' She spoke almost to herself.

'I think if he had wanted to marry her he would have done so years ago. She flies backwards and forwards to see him all the time. He must have had countless opportunities to commit to her. But he's asking you. That must mean something.'

'I think it just means that he puts Liam first in his life.'

'Well, that's good…isn't it?'

'It's good in some ways…' Gemma shrugged and lowered her voice to a husky whisper. 'But I have needs too, Mum.' She remembered the way Marcus had so coolly set out to seduce her yesterday, the way he'd kissed her and the heat and passion of his caresses, then the controlled way he had been able to move back from her when he had proved his point. 'I can't marry someone who doesn't love me.'

'So you've turned him down?'

'I haven't given him an answer yet. But it has to be no. He thinks he can have what he wants, that because he has money and power I'll say yes. He's tried to buy me with a fabulous job, with the fact that I'll be in a lovely home with a great lifestyle.'

'Sounds good to me,' her mother said dryly.

'Well, I won't be bought.' Gemma turned away and searched her pockets for some change for the coffee machine. 'I don't need him. He can go to Italy or go to hell for all I care.' She put the coins into the slot with a shaking hand.

'But you love him,' her mother said quietly beside her. 'You've always loved him.'

'No, I don't,' Gemma said fiercely.

'You can lie to yourself as much as you like, Gemma, but you don't fool me.' Joanne's voice was softly insistent. 'I know you. I've seen the way you look at him, the expression on your face at the mere mention of his name. You've never stopped loving him.'

'That's not true.' Gemma's voice trembled alarmingly and the buttons on the coffee machine suddenly blurred behind a mist of tears.

'If you turn him down, what will you be staying in London for?' Joanne continued persistently. 'Not for Richard, that's for sure. Your feelings for him are lukewarm at best.'

'I like Richard,' Gemma maintained stubbornly.

'If you say no to Marcus you will wake up to regret it. Okay, he hasn't told you he loves you, but he has asked you to marry him—*twice*. Maybe in view of the fact that you still have feelings for him, and the fact that Liam adores him, it's time you threw away that foolish pride of yours and met him halfway.'

The words were tough and uncompromising and they tore into Gemma's consciousness with brutal force.

'And, just for the record, I think Marcus cares about you deeply. There's a certain inflection in his voice when he asks about you sometimes—'

'You're really grasping at straws now, Mum,' Gemma said with a shake of her head.

'Marriage isn't all roses around the door, Gemma. But I think if you and Marcus worked at it, you could have something really special.'

'Hi, Gemma,' Richard's cheerful voice called to her down the corridor and she turned to see him heading in their direction with a huge bouquet of flowers and a big box of chocolates in his arms.

'How's Liam? Everything is okay, isn't it?' He looked at her in alarm as he noticed the pallor of her skin and the bright glitter of her eyes.

'Yes, he's fine. In fact, they've just told me they will be discharging him today. I was on my way to phone you.'

'Gemma, this must all have been a terrible ordeal for you.' He put his arms around her and gathered her close in against him. For a second the scent of lilies and carnations assailed her.

Richard was a good man, she thought, decent and kind…why couldn't she be in love with him? But the fact remained that there was no flutter of excitement at being in his arms, no fierce thrill of pleasure at all. The heart could be very stupid, she thought angrily.

As she pulled back from him she saw Marcus walking down the corridor, noted the dark gleam of derision in his eyes as he witnessed their embrace. She remembered how he had poured scorn on her relationship with Richard the other day. What was it he had said? *'Richard strikes me as a trifle weak…not the type to be able to handle you at all. And certainly not the type to turn you on.'*

The arrogance of that remark seared through her angrily. Obviously Marcus believed he had no real competition. That conceited confidence fired Gemma's blood and made her impulsively reach to kiss Richard on the lips as he handed her the flowers.

'Thanks, Richard,' she whispered huskily.

'Well, you're welcome.' Richard blushed slightly and

looked extraordinarily pleased. And suddenly Gemma wished she hadn't done that.

'The chocolates are for Liam.' Richard shyly passed them over to her as well.

'Thanks—you shouldn't have.' Gemma felt flustered as Marcus reached her side.

'Morning, everyone.' He smiled around at them all, his manner relaxed. Then, much to Gemma's consternation, he reached and put an arm around her waist, drawing her close towards him with an easy familiarity. 'Good news—I've just been speaking to the doctor and he's about to discharge our son.'

The touch of his hand and the scent of his aftershave sent her heart into a frenzied overdrive. She noticed how Richard and her mother took in the closeness of their stance and she wanted to wrench herself crossly away from him but she didn't get the chance because Marcus had already moved to shake Richard's hand. 'Good of you to come down,' he said. 'Sorry you've had a bit of a wasted journey.'

'Doesn't matter,' Richard said pleasantly. 'Gemma was just telling me the good news. I'll stick my head around the door and say hello to him anyway.'

'Liam will be delighted.' Gemma moved to take hold of Richard's arm, steering him firmly away from Marcus. She wished she hadn't caught her mother's eye just at that moment, because it was obvious from the expression on her face that she knew exactly why Gemma was gushing over Richard and she wasn't impressed.

Liam was pleased to see Richard but he was more taken with the fact that his father was back and had brought him a new pair of pyjamas with pictures of an

Italian football team on it. 'Wow, Daddy! Wow, thanks!' he kept saying.

'I thought you'd be in here another night,' Marcus said with a grin. 'But you'll just have to save them for home now.'

'Can Mummy and I come back to your house tonight?' Liam asked suddenly.

'Liam, I've told you that you are not going to Daddy this weekend,' Gemma cut in swiftly, trying to ignore the awkward atmosphere that suddenly seemed to have descended with that question, the watchful eyes of her mother and Richard, and the gleam in Marcus's gaze as he glanced over at her.

'Aw, but Mum!'

'Not today, Liam.' His father cut across him firmly. 'But soon.'

Why did he have to say that? Gemma wondered angrily. He just had to tack the word, 'soon' on, to show her that he was going to win this battle of attrition.

'I suppose our dinner date is out of the question tonight?' Richard asked her quietly.

'Well, I don't want to leave Liam at the moment, Richard.' She paused, wondering if she should ask him around to the house for dinner, but somehow she couldn't face the thought of making polite conversation. She wanted to concentrate on Liam and think seriously about where their future lay…here in London, or in Italy with Marcus. 'Let's make it next week instead.' Conscious of the fact that Marcus was listening she tacked on, 'That way we can really relax and enjoy ourselves.'

'Okay,' Richard agreed with her easily. 'Next week it is.' He turned the conversation towards Liam, asking him what it had been like to be in hospital.

Gemma listened to the conversation. Richard was quite serious with him and Liam answered politely, a solemn expression on his little face. It was quite different when Marcus spoke, making Liam chuckle as if he'd said the funniest things in the world.

Her eyes moved between the two men. Richard was dressed sombrely in a pale grey shirt and black trousers. Marcus was wearing jeans and a blue denim shirt that was open at the neck. He looked confident and relaxed, and extremely sexy. Her eyes lingered on his hands, remembering how they had moved over her so possessively.

'Gemma… Gemma.' Her mother reached over and touched her arm. 'I'm going to go now. I'll ring you later.'

'Oh, right.' Gemma hoped her mother hadn't noticed that she had been staring at Marcus. 'Thanks for everything, Mum.'

'Okay.' She leaned forward to kiss her daughter on the cheek. 'Don't make any rash decisions,' she whispered.

Gemma smiled at her and concluded that was code for 'Don't turn Marcus down'.

'If you're going, I'll give you a lift, Joanne,' Richard said, also getting to his feet. 'I'm going in that direction anyway.'

'That's very kind of you, Richard.' Joanne smiled, then waved over at Marcus and gave Liam a hug. 'Be good for your mum.'

'I'll see you Monday morning,' Richard said as he bent to kiss Gemma goodbye.

'I'm not sure, Richard. I'll have to see how Liam is.'

'But you've got your interview on Monday!' Richard reminded her with a frown and she felt her skin overheat with embarrassment as she realized she had forgotten all about the interview. 'Unless Marcus is going to arrange for it to be rescheduled for you?'

'That's not up to me, Richard,' Marcus said smoothly. 'That call is down to Henry Perkins. I'm leaving the day-to-day running of the magazine to him.'

'Well, you'd better give him a ring if you're not going to make it, Gemma,' Richard said with a worried shake of his head. 'You've worked too long and too hard to throw away the opportunity of your promotion now.'

'Don't worry, Richard. I'll sort it out,' Gemma said quietly.

As the door closed behind her mother and Richard, Gemma glared over at Marcus. She didn't believe for one moment that he was leaving the appointment of the new editor entirely up to Henry Perkins. He was just being deliberately obtuse because he had no intention of allowing her to get the job there.

'Don't look at me like that, Gemma. The job interviews are nothing to do with me.'

'Of course they are something to do with you. You own the magazine!'

'So what are you saying? That you want me to pull strings for you?' he asked calmly.

'You know that's not what I mean. I'm saying that I don't want you to interfere in any way.'

'That's fine then, because I don't intend to.'

Gemma didn't believe him, but there was no time to say anything further because Liam's doctor arrived at that moment to check him over.

'He's much better.' The doctor smiled over at them both as he finished making some notes on his clipboard. 'Your son is quite a fighter—his immune system kicked in and fought off the infection much faster than I had expected. But you need to keep a close eye on him now for the next few months. Just to make sure we don't have any recurrence.'

'You mean the virus could come back?' Gemma was horrified.

'I don't think it's likely but he is still a little under par. Nothing to worry about unduly.' The doctor ruffled Liam's hair playfully. 'With a bit of TLC from mum and dad, a bit of fresh air and good food, you should be right as rain in no time, Liam.' He smiled over at Gemma. 'Just keep an eye on him and bring him along to his GP in six weeks for a check-up. I'm sure he'll give you the all clear.'

'We will do that, Doctor. Thank you,' Marcus said with a nod.

'Can I go home now?' Liam asked hopefully.

'Yes, darling, you can come home,' Gemma said thankfully.

Marcus helped pack up Liam's belongings while Gemma changed him out of his pyjamas.

'Have you got your car here?' Marcus asked her as he lifted Liam up into his arms.

She shook her head. 'I got a taxi.'

'Right, we'll go back in mine,' he said, picking up Liam's holdall with his spare hand. 'Come on, let's get out of here.'

Gemma didn't argue with him. She wasn't up to getting taxis, she just wanted to get Liam home as soon as possible.

She sat silently as Marcus drove them back, only half listening to Liam's cheerful chatter in the back. Her mind was focusing on the doctor's words. The fact that the virus could return was frightening.

'Are you okay?' Marcus glanced over at her.

'Yes, I'm just thinking about the doctor's advice. I think I'll take next week off work to keep an eye on Liam.'

'I'll come over and stay with him on Monday if you want to attend your interview.'

The casual offer took her by surprise. 'You'd really do that?'

'I said so, didn't I?'

'It's just…well, I didn't think you wanted me to have that job.'

'I don't.' He glanced sideways at her and his dark eyes seemed to slice straight into her very soul. 'You know what I want. I made that clear yesterday. But it's your decision. If you want to go for that interview on Monday, then go. I'll be there for Liam.'

'Thanks, that's a kind offer—'

He frowned at that. 'He's my responsibility too, Gemma. It's only right that I help out…at least for as long as I can.'

She knew that was a veiled reference to the fact that he would be leaving soon. And the awareness of just how deeply that was going to affect them all was deeply disturbing.

'If you had let me finish, I was going to say that it was a kind offer, but I won't be taking you up on it, because I've decided not to apply for the job after all.'

Marcus looked over at her with a raised eyebrow. 'Does that mean you are going to accept my offer?'

The quietly asked question seemed to reverberate in the silence of the car.

'It means that I've been thinking about what the doctor said and I suddenly realize just how unimportant work is compared to my son's health.' Gemma looked away from him down at her hands, clasped tightly in her lap. 'And I've decided that I don't want promotion—in fact, if anything, I think I should be downsizing my job, so I can spend more time with Liam.'

'That's a mighty big decision.'

'I know…' She smiled shakily. 'But being in that hospital has made me take a long hard look at my priorities, and listening to that doctor just now scared me. Liam is the most precious thing in my life…the job means nothing beside that.'

Marcus pulled the car to a standstill in front of her house. 'Does that mean you are going to come to Italy with me?' he asked softly.

When she didn't answer him immediately, he reached and took hold of her hand. The touch of his skin against hers sent shivers of feeling running through her.

'The job at *Élan* doesn't become vacant until mid-September. So you could take the summer to relax at the villa with Liam, decide what you want to do about work at your leisure.'

Gemma felt confusion strike and suddenly she didn't know what to think any more. The offer sounded remarkably tempting—and did he mean that she could take the summer to consider whether or not she would marry him?

'Are you going to Italy, Daddy?' Liam's little voice in the back of the car brought them both up with a start. He'd been sitting so quietly that they had forgotten he might be listening.

'I'm just talking about it now, Liam,' Marcus said gently.

'Is it business?' Liam asked. He was used to his father making short business trips to the continent.

'We'll talk about it later, Liam,' his father said firmly.

Gemma liked the way he didn't try to lie to him. In

fact, she liked everything about the way he acted around his son.

Marcus turned his attention back to her.

'Why don't you invite me to stay for dinner and we can discuss this further?'

A cheer of enthusiasm from the back seat met the matter-of-fact question. 'Yeah, Daddy can stay for dinner and I can show him how I've put up my train set.'

Marcus looked at her with a gleam of amusement in his eyes now. 'So what do you say?'

Gemma only hesitated fractionally and then shrugged. 'Well, it looks like I've been outvoted. So you'd better come in.'

It seemed strange being downstairs in the kitchen knowing Marcus was upstairs with Liam. She could hear the distant rattle of the toy train and Liam's laughter, and it made her smile with pleasure. It was good having him home, and hearing him so happy was music to her ears. She was never going to take things like that for granted again, she thought.

The fact that Liam was in extra high spirits because his father was here couldn't be ignored either. If she let Marcus walk away from them her son was going to be devastated. So what should she do?

Gemma turned on the stove and then busied herself making a salad. Thinking too deeply about Marcus brought confusion, but it was something that she had to face. Should she go to Italy?

Marriage without love wasn't an option, she told herself sternly. And she didn't love him…yesterday had been a moment of weakness. It had been about sex…nothing else.

Marcus left Liam playing and went downstairs to see

Gemma. He noticed that she had put the flowers from Richard in a crystal bowl in the hall. Their scent was overpowering, almost as overpowering as the fury that had assailed him when he had watched Richard taking her into his arms. She was his, he thought angrily now, and he was damned if he was going to lose her to the likes of Richard Barry.

He paused in the open doorway to the kitchen. Gemma was standing at the kitchen counter, busy chopping peppers on a wooden board and then sliding them into a sizzling pan on the stove. She seemed immersed in the task, completely lost in thought and obviously not aware of his presence at all. What was she thinking about? he wondered.

He noticed the way the evening rays of sunshine were slanting through the kitchen window behind her, capturing the gold lights in her blonde hair, making it shimmer as she turned her head. Noticed the perfection of her skin, the dark sweep of her lashes, the soft curve of her lips. Then his eyes moved lower to the way her blue dress clung to the curves of her body and he remembered the heat and passion that had flared between them yesterday. It had taken all his willpower to be able to draw back from her. He had wanted to follow through and take her completely…he wanted that now, the need for her so strong it was burning him away inside.

Surely she couldn't have responded to him like that if she were in love with Richard? The thought crept into his mind that she had responded to him passionately once before when she had been in love with someone else. His own brother, no less.

He remembered Freddie's hurt expression when he had told him he'd been seeing her. Remembered the pain in his words. *'How could you do this to me, Marcus?*

She's mine, God damn it…she's the woman I'm going to marry…'

He hadn't seen that one coming, Marcus reminded himself brutally. When he had gone to his brother to ask him why he was taking Gemma to Helene's wedding, he had half-expected Freddie to admit he fancied her— or was hoping for a relationship stronger than friendship. That there was already a relationship going on had stunned him.

'Of course, you know why she's seeing you. It's to further her career, nothing more. She loves me… She's saving herself for me and the only reason we haven't slept together yet is because we want our wedding night to be special.'

At least he knew Gemma wasn't looking to further her career with him this time, Marcus reminded himself, trying to cut the painful memories of the terrible argument with Freddie. He had loved his brother and the knowledge of what he had done to him still tore him apart with grief and guilt. Sometimes in his nightmares he could still see his brother's face, his eyes glimmering with rage, with unshed tears of emotion.

For a long time after Freddie's death the conversation had haunted him, and he had hardly been able to bear to look at Gemma, he had been so burdened with guilt. And yet he had never stopped wanting her…desiring her…dreaming of her naked in his arms. When he had seen her out with Richard a few weeks ago it had focused his mind sharply. She hadn't seen him. They had been leaving a restaurant together, Richard's arm firmly around her waist. But the sight of them together had been a shock. And suddenly he had known with a searing clarity that he couldn't afford to have regrets about the past. He had to look to the future, and he saw that future with Gemma and Liam.

He moved and she looked up in surprise. 'How long have you been standing there?'

'Not long.' He walked further into the room and came to stand behind her, watching her as she worked. 'Do you need a hand with anything?'

'No, everything is under control, thanks.' She wished that were true. The food might be under control but her body temperature and her emotions definitely weren't. He was too close to her and she was acutely conscious of his body just a whisper away from hers. All she would have to do was turn around and she would be in his arms.

'What are you making?'

'Nothing exciting, I'm afraid, as I haven't had a chance to go shopping. Just pasta and a side salad.' It was difficult keeping her voice steady and light.

'Sounds good to me.' His breath tickled on the side of her face as he reached across and stole a piece of raw pepper. He didn't touch her but her body was so acutely tuned to the heat of his that it made every nerve ending tingle. In that instant the need to turn around and melt into him was so powerful it was almost overwhelming.

Her mother's words taunted her loudly in her mind. *You love him. You've always loved him… It's time you threw away that foolish pride of yours and met him half-way.*

'So what were you thinking about as you chopped away so industriously?' he asked, still not moving back from her.

'Not a lot.' She wondered how he would feel if she were to tell him she'd been thinking about her body's clamouring need to be held by him? He'd probably be arrogantly pleased, knowing Marcus, she reminded herself sharply.

'Did you mean it when you said you didn't want the promotion with *Modern Times*?'

The serious turn to his questions made her heart miss a beat. 'Yes, I did.'

'So will you come away with me, Gemma?' He put his hands at either side of her on the counter. 'You'll love living in Italy, I promise you.'

Gemma squeezed her eyes tightly closed.

'And Liam will love it. He's already almost fluent in the language, he'll be completely at home…and he'll thrive there.'

Still she didn't answer.

'So what do you think…will you say yes to my proposal?' The words were silkily smooth.

She had given up all pretence of work now and her hands clenched into tight impotent fists at her side.

He turned the stove off. 'Gemma? It will be the perfect arrangement.' He whispered the words close to her ear; his breath tickled and tantalized the skin on her neck.

He touched her then, one hand lightly on her shoulder as he turned her around to face him. Then he put a hand under her chin, tipping her head up so that she was forced to meet the darkness of his eyes. His thumb moved to stroke silkily across the soft fullness of her lower lip. The butterfly caress teased the sensory nerve endings, making her tremble inside. She longed for him to kiss her, longed for it so badly that it was like a deep ache inside.

'I think we are mature enough to make a marriage work. We both know what we want…' His hand moved to stroke a stray strand of hair away from her face, tucking it behind one ear. She wanted to tell him not to touch her; the sensation of his skin against hers was exquisite torture.

She loved him. The realisation suddenly screamed through her. *She adored him.*

She could lie to herself as much as she wanted but the truth was that she had been lost as soon as he had touched her again, as soon as she had been held fleetingly in his arms that day by Liam's bedside. All the memories that she had tried so desperately to close out had started to flood in again. And she realized now that her mother was right, she had never really lost her love of Marcus, she had just succeeded in masking it.

Yesterday, as soon as his hands had touched her body, she had been right back to where she had started with him five and a half years ago, totally and utterly under his spell. After all these years of telling herself that she was over him, it was a devastating admission to have to make and it made her incredibly angry with herself for being so weak where he was concerned.

'I never envisioned myself marrying for any other reason than love,' she murmured unsteadily.

'Do you love Richard?' His voice became sharper.

She shrugged and then deliberately lied. 'Maybe…'

'That's a very half-hearted declaration of love,' he grated derisively.

'Yes, well, Liam doesn't have a strong bond with Richard. And I'm a parent first, Marcus, that tends to change the way you view relationships.'

Marcus nodded. 'Yes, I realize that.'

The dry words sidetracked her somewhat. 'Is that the reason you haven't got married before now?'

'It has a bearing on it, yes.' His eyes moved towards

her lips and a flare of desire shimmered through her with sudden intensity.

'If I did agree to marry you, it would only be for Liam's sake…nothing else.' Her voice trembled precariously.

'Of course.' He smiled. 'Does that mean your answer is yes?'

She didn't reply to that. 'I don't want Liam to be without his father, you see…I can't bear the knowledge that if I turn you down I'll hurt him badly.' Her heart was thundering against her chest. She was aware she was desperately making excuses both to herself and him. She hated the weakness inside that desperately wanted to say yes, when she knew the answer should be no.

'Gemma, get to the bottom line.' His voice was abrupt; his eyes seemed locked on her lips. 'Will you marry me?'

'Yes…' The word was a mere whisper in the silence between them. She saw the flare of triumph in his eyes and hated herself for caving in so easily, but she couldn't help it. She wanted him with all her heart. She loved him.

He cupped her face in both his hands. 'You won't regret it. This is the right thing for Liam…for all of us.'

The feel of his hands against her skin was like a brand of possession.

Her breathing felt tight and constricted as he lowered his head towards hers and she realized he was going to kiss her.

His lips, soft and persuasive against hers, created the most intensely erotic sensation. It was as if he were laying claim to her, possessing her hungrily, and her body clamoured for so much more. Her breasts longed to feel his hands; her skin tingled with the need to be closer.

But then abruptly he stepped back. 'We'll leave for Italy next week and get married over there. If I apply for a special licence now that should mean we can have the ceremony within about ten days or so.'

'Ten days?' Her eyes widened. 'That's too soon!'

'No, it's not.' He stroked the side of her face and the soft touch distracted her. 'We've wasted enough time.'

'We should wait and get married here in London...' She was half panicking now, scared of what she was doing, but the other part of her was breathless with excitement. It was one thing agreeing in theory to a marriage without love—was she really going to go through with it?

'I know you'll want your mother and friends to attend and that's no problem. I'll get the air tickets. But we'll be married in Italy, Gemma.'

His voice was firmly decisive. Her senses were in complete disarray from the kiss, from the speed that he was taking things...from the fact that she wanted him to make love to her and talk about wedding dates later.

'I don't know, it seems a bit fast.'

His gaze took in the swollen softness of her lips, the huge blue eyes. 'And as I said, we've wasted enough time. I want you now...'

'Mummy, I bumped my elbow on the staircase.'

The little voice in the doorway took them both by surprise.

'Did you, darling?' She moved past Marcus to go and pick the child up. 'Where does it hurt?' she asked him gently.

'Just here.' He pointed to his arm and watched as she pushed up his sleeve to inspect the damage. 'No harm done. Just a little bump, I think,' she said softly and kissed him. 'There...does that feel better?'

He nodded.

'You look sleepy, darling.' She pushed a tender hand through his hair. 'It's been a long day, hasn't it?'

Liam nodded again and looked over at his dad. 'You're still staying for tea though, aren't you, Daddy?' he asked him anxiously.

Marcus nodded and came closer. 'In fact, you're going to be seeing a lot more of me from now on, Liam.'

Gemma felt her heart starting to bounce unsteadily again in her chest as she met his eyes, saw the question there. 'Shall I tell him?' he asked her softly.

She hesitated. As soon as they told Liam there would be no going back on her decision, she knew that.

'Gemma?' He looked at her with an intensity that tore at her heart. And she nodded.

'Yes, let's tell him.' She cuddled Liam closer to her, taking comfort in the warm little arms that stole around her neck, and in the fact that this was going to make her son very happy.

CHAPTER EIGHT

WHEN Gemma woke up that morning her first thought was that this was her last morning as a single woman.

Outside she could hear the distant rumble of traffic heading towards the centre of Rome. She glanced around the unfamiliar bedroom with its floral wallpaper and heavy wooden furniture and saw her wedding dress hanging on the back of the wardrobe, a delicious pale cream silk that was stylishly understated. Next to it, on the floor, her suitcase sat neatly packed, ready to be taken up to Marcus's villa.

Thinking about the momentous step that lay before her, Gemma felt a tingle of nerves which seemed to work its way up from her toes through her entire body. The alarm clock rang shrilly in the silence of the room. She reached out and switched it off.

Was she doing the right thing? The question had tormented her through the last two weeks. But everything had moved so quickly that there hadn't been a lot of time to think. She remembered the reaction in the office when she had told them she was leaving. Everyone had been shocked, but no one more so than Richard. Just thinking about the look on his face made her sad all over again.

Hurting Richard had not been easy. He had been such a good friend to her, especially over the last couple of months, but at least their relationship, if you could really call it that, had only just started. He had been disappointed and upset, had told her he thought she was making a big mistake rushing into marriage. But they had parted as friends and she had promised to keep in touch.

Gemma got out of bed and pulled back the curtains. The morning sunlight caught the engagement ring on her finger and it splintered into a myriad of dazzling colours. Marcus had presented her with the square-cut diamond solitaire just before they left London last week, but she still wasn't used to wearing it, was still overwhelmed by its beauty.

Her eyes moved to admire the view from her bedroom window; the city of Rome was bathed in the soft golden light of morning. This was the room that she had stayed in when she came to attend Helene's wedding. It was strange being back in Marcus's father's house. The last time she had stood at this window she had felt like her heart was breaking. Who would have thought that she would return, and that she would stand here and admire this view on the day she would marry Marcus?

She put on her dressing-gown and padded quietly across the hall to peep into Liam's room. He was still fast asleep, which wasn't surprising as it had been almost ten-thirty last night before she had been able to settle him down. Excitement had been bubbling inside him and he had talked incessantly, about the wedding, about living in Italy. And the fact that his father had arrived just as she had got him into bed hadn't helped.

'Isn't it bad luck to see the bride on the night before the wedding?' Gemma had asked when she had gone downstairs and bumped into him coming through the front door.

'I'm not the superstitious type.' He had grinned.

'Well, I am,' she had said firmly. 'I never walk under ladders, or put shoes on a table.'

'Well, they are just common sense precautions.'

'So is not letting the groom over the threshold the night before the wedding.'

She didn't know why she had pretended not to be glad to see him, when in reality all she had wanted was for him to take her into his arms and kiss her senseless. But it was a game she had played since accepting his proposal. She had too much pride to let him know that her heart went into overdrive at the mere sight of him.

Marcus had just smiled and stepped past her. 'Well, I won't keep you long. I just thought I'd call and say goodnight to Liam—is he still up?'

'He is now,' Gemma had said as she heard his footsteps on the landing and then the excited squeals of 'Daddy, Daddy, Daddy!'

Anyone would have thought Liam hadn't seen his dad in a fortnight instead of that afternoon. Which, she supposed, went to prove how much she was doing the right thing where her child was concerned. But as far as *she* was concerned, Gemma still wasn't at all sure.

There hadn't been a chance for them to be alone together since the moment when she had accepted his proposal. In one way it was a good thing because emotionally it helped her to keep her guard up. Marcus was so coolly confident about everything and she couldn't let him know that deep down she was scared to death…that she loved him so much it hurt. She had her pride. In fact, it was probably the only thing she had left. Marcus was taking everything else over, forcefully and absolutely.

He'd taken charge of closing up the house, arranging shipping and storage for certain items. He'd arranged for her to leave work without having to serve out the necessary notice. Everything had swept ahead with the force of a tidal wave.

She had said as much to him last night before he had left.

'Having last-minute doubts?' he had asked quietly, turning to look at her.

'Yes, I am, millions of them,' she had said honestly. 'What about you?'

He had smiled. And something about the way his eyes had raked over her face, lingering on her lips, had sent prickles of awareness racing through her.

'Not one. I know absolutely that this is the right thing.'

Those confident words echoed in her mind now as she wandered back to her bedroom and the en-suite bathroom to have her shower. Of course Marcus would feel like that. He was getting Liam…the one thing that made his life complete.

All Marcus's family were thrilled about the wedding, and they doted on Liam. His grandfather Giorgio Rossini in particular was crazy about him. He had been the one who had insisted they stay here before the ceremony. 'I want to get to know my grandson better,' he had said firmly. 'There has been too much distance between us for too long.'

Liam had been a little shy at first and had clung to her. He didn't really know his grandfather very well, having only seen him on a few occasions when Giorgio had visited London. But after the first day it was as if Liam had always known this house and these people. He was running around playing with his cousins and laughing with his grandfather quite happily.

Gemma raised her head to the pummelling pressure of hot water. The house was filled with joy and excitement and it was hard not to get carried away by it all, to believe that this marriage was real and that Marcus really did love her. But deep down she knew that wasn't true. The fact was that her emotions were a lot like the house she had left behind in London, shrouded under dustsheets. She was frightened of looking too deeply under the covers. Scared to examine this forthcoming marriage too closely in case she might not be able to deal with what she found. For instance, she hadn't dared to question Marcus about Sophia, in case she didn't like his answer.

She kept telling herself that the woman would be out of Marcus's life for good now that he was marrying her. But was that the case? Maybe Marcus envisaged some kind of open marriage, where he kept a mistress? Then he'd have the best of all worlds…his family and his lover.

Gemma snapped off the shower and swiftly pushed the idea away. Sophia would surely never tolerate that, not when she'd had hopes of marrying him herself one day. And anyway, Marcus had said he wanted to give their marriage a real chance of working; he'd hardly say that and keep a mistress. She had to put thoughts like that out of her head because they didn't help.

At one-thirty today she would officially become Mrs Marcus Rossini and then everything would start to come right in her world. She would be with the one man she had always loved. And okay, maybe he didn't love her, but she had enough love for the two of them and she would make this marriage work.

As she stepped back into her bedroom there was a knock at the door and Marcus's sister Helene came in with a cup of tea for her. 'How are you feeling?' she asked with a smile.

'Nervous,' Gemma admitted wryly.

Helene laughed. She was a very beautiful woman with

long dark hair and smiling dark eyes. 'Well, if it makes
you feel better, I think Marcus is nervous as well. I rang
the villa a few moments ago to see how he was going
on and his housekeeper told me he'd gone out.'

'Out? At eight in the morning?' Gemma wondered
suddenly if Marcus was having doubts about this marriage as well. Maybe that cool confident manner of his
was just an act. Maybe deep down he was just as ap-
prehensive and uncertain as she was.

'Oh, he'll be down at the stables having an early
morning ride.' Helene grinned. 'He always does that
when something important is on the horizon. The day he
took over the business from Papà he was up at dawn
and out riding for a couple of hours. He says it helps
him focus on the day ahead.'

Gemma frowned. It suddenly struck her how little she
really knew about Marcus. Even though they had a child
together, it was a bit like marrying a stranger. She knew
he was a good father, an excellent businessman, and she
knew she liked his family. But the man himself was still
an enigma to her.

'Oh, by the way.' Helene reached into the pocket of
her dress and brought out a small flat box. 'Marcus asked
me to give you that this morning.' With a smile Helene
put the gift down on the dressing table and headed for
the door. 'I'd better go. I said I'd accompany Papà to
the airport to pick up your guests, give them a proper
Italian welcome.'

Gemma smiled. 'Thanks, Helene.' She had only invited her mother, her best friend, Jane, and her partner,
Steve, to the wedding because she had wanted to keep
the occasion low key. It was a forlorn hope, because the
Rossini family alone would probably pack the church.

As the door closed behind her future sister-in-law,

Gemma reached to open the box. Inside there was the most stunning square-cut diamond on a white gold chain and a note that said simply,

Thought this might look good on you, Marcus.

Not *love* Marcus…just 'Marcus'.

Gemma fastened the diamond around her neck. It looked fabulous. But she would have traded all the diamonds in the world if he had just written that one extra little word on the card.

The festivities for the wedding seemed to be underway even before Gemma had put on her wedding dress. The large double doors leading out to the secluded back garden were open and huge tables groaning with food had been laid out on the patio. People seemed to be arriving in droves and presents and cards were mounting up on the trestle tables in the hallway.

'The Italians certainly know how to party.' Her mother laughed as she came upstairs to help Gemma with the last-minute attention to details. 'I don't know how anyone will be able to eat at the reception after all that food downstairs—' She stopped abruptly as she saw her daughter in her wedding dress. 'You look gorgeous.' She sighed. 'An absolute picture.'

The dress did do incredible things for Gemma's figure. It hugged her tiny waist and skimmed over her curves in a most flattering way. The soft cream silk made her skin look luminous. Her hair was softly caught up with cream roses and around her neck was the necklace from Marcus.

'The car is here,' Helene called excitedly up the stairs and Gemma felt another flutter of nerves.

'Where is Liam?' she asked her mother.

'He left for the chapel with his uncles and cousins five minutes ago.'

Gemma nodded. 'Then I suppose it's time I followed him.'

As the limousine slowly rounded the corner towards the church the first person she saw was Liam, standing at the bottom of the steps. He looked adorable in his dark morning suit, his hair neatly brushed back from his face, and he waved with excitement as he saw the car.

The limousine pulled up beside them and the driver jumped out to open the door for her. As she stepped out on to the pavement her eyes connected with Marcus. Why was he standing outside the church? she wondered anxiously. Was something wrong?

He looked awesome in his morning suit. The penetrating dark eyes that held hers sent shivers of excitement and desire rushing through her.

'What are you doing out here?' she whispered. 'Shouldn't you be inside the church?'

'I wanted to see you arrive. You look beautiful, Gemma,' he said softly, his eyes raking over her body in a possessive way.

She smiled at him and suddenly her doubts were forgotten.

'Daddy said I was to give you this,' Liam said and brought out a single red rose from behind his back.

'Thank you, darling.' Gemma crouched down beside him to take it and then gave him a kiss.

'Hey, that's my kiss you're stealing, Liam,' Marcus said, putting a hand on his son's shoulder, and Liam giggled happily. Gemma straightened and looked up into Marcus's eyes. 'But I'll claim my kiss later,' he said huskily.

And suddenly the thought of the night ahead, of being

in his arms and having him make love to her, burnt through her consciousness.

He held out his hand towards her. 'Are you ready for this?' he asked.

She hesitated for just one second before placing her hand in his. 'As ready as I'll ever be,' she said, trying to feign a lightness of tone, trying to pretend that the touch of his hand against hers wasn't sending darts of electricity dancing through her.

'Hey, Marcus, you should be waiting for us inside!' His father stepped forward with an impatient shake of his head. 'I'm the one who is walking into the chapel with Gemma, you should be waiting with nervous anticipation by the altar.'

'Just going…' Marcus smiled at Gemma. 'See you in a moment.'

'Honestly, my son always has to do things his way,' Georgio said teasingly.

'Yes, I've noticed.' Gemma smiled.

The small church was packed with members of the Rossini family. But Gemma only had eyes for Marcus as she walked towards him down the aisle.

Suddenly this felt so right…

As she reached Marcus's side he took hold of her hand and she felt as if she had arrived somewhere that she should have been a long time ago.

She looked up at him and smiled and he squeezed her hand. 'I'll look after you, Gemma…I promise,' he whispered huskily.

Afterwards, when she looked back, those words were like part of the ceremony. The solemn look in his eyes, the pressure of his skin against hers.

Then the priest was welcoming them and the service began. Gemma's voice was hushed and not altogether steady as she repeated her vows. Marcus, on the other hand, was firm and decisive.

He slid the gold wedding band on to her finger resolutely.

'I now pronounce you man and wife.' The priest said the words in Italian and then repeated them in English. 'You may kiss the bride.'

It was hard to believe that such a short period of time could change someone's life so radically. Gemma looked up into Marcus's eyes with a feeling almost of unreality. Maybe this wasn't really happening to her, she thought dazedly. Maybe this was all a dream. Then Marcus leaned closer and his lips covered hers, not in a gentle way but in a fiercely possessive kiss that claimed her totally as his. And as she felt the answering surge of blazing heat inside her she knew with certainty that this was no dream.

Outside in the full glare of the sunshine they were showered with confetti, and then they paused for photographs before climbing back into a stretch limousine.

'Well, we did it,' Marcus said with a wry grin as he looked over at her.

'Yes, we did.' Gemma waved at Liam who was going to follow behind them in the car with Marcus's father and her mother.

She settled back into her seat and looked over at Marcus.

'You make a very lovely bride, Mrs Rossini.' He smiled.

'Thank you.' Her heart missed several beats. 'And thank you for the necklace. It's lovely.' She touched the diamond around her neck. 'I feel quite embarrassed because I didn't buy you anything.'

He smiled at that. 'You can give me your present tonight,' he said in a low teasing tone and smiled as he saw the flare of colour in her cheeks.

As she looked away from him he reached out and tipped her chin upwards so that she was forced to look at him. 'And I'm looking forward to unwrapping it very slowly,' he added softly. 'Savouring every moment... In fact, maybe I won't be able to contain myself until to-night. I think I've waited long enough...' He leaned closer. She could smell the scent of his cologne, mixed with the scent of the roses in her bouquet. Then his mouth covered hers, plundering the softness of her lips with delicious intent. Her stomach dipped as if she were experiencing the thrill of a fairground ride.

She felt his hands moving up over the bodice of her dress and she longed to feel them more intimately.

'We shouldn't, Marcus...' she whispered unsteadily. 'There's the driver and...people will see us....'

'To hell with people seeing. If I want to kiss my wife, I will.' Marcus grinned, his fingers stroking over the firmness of her body, noting the instinctive rise of her breast beneath his touch.

Then she was kissing him back with heated passion.

The loud blare of horns made her pull away from him.

Marcus laughed as she looked out into the crowded streets to see if there had been an accident. 'Relax. It's just people wishing us well. We'll probably be driving all the way out towards the restaurant accompanied by that noise.'

He was right; the uproarious din of horns continued as they left the city and headed out into the hills. And suddenly Gemma was reminded of Helene's wedding day. The Italian countryside bathed in sunshine, just like this, the fields of corn ripening to pale green gold, scarlet poppies lining the roadsides and cutting swathes through the lush meadows. Only then she had been sitting next to Freddie, painfully aware that the car ahead of them in the convoy held Marcus and Sophia.

'So, where were we…?' Marcus murmured, reaching to touch her again.

'We really shouldn't, Marcus.' She pulled away from him. 'That should wait until later…' She tried to force herself to be sensible but all her emotions were crying out for him to continue.

Marcus smiled. 'I suppose you are right.' Despite the words his hand moved teasingly to stroke the side of her face. 'But it's a pity because you look so ravishing in that dress that right at this moment…I really…want an aperitif…'

He leaned closer and his lips crushed against hers again and she found herself kissing him back hungrily. Her bouquet fell to the floor as the touch of his hand became more heated, his kisses more intrusive.

Then abruptly he pulled away from her and looked out of the window. 'But you are right, there is no time for this now. We'll be at the restaurant soon.'

The words made her hastily try to straighten her dress, smoothing down the ruffles in the silk with a shaking hand.

Marcus watched her with a gleam of amusement in his eye.

'It's not funny,' she said unsteadily, fastening up the top button on her bodice. 'I've got visions of the car pulling up surrounded by all your family.'

He laughed softly. 'Relax, they can't see in here anyway. It's tinted glass.'

Marcus picked up her bouquet and handed it to her. 'How's my hair?' she asked him nervously.

He smiled. 'You look gorgeous…tasted gorgeous as well.'

'Very funny. You've probably smudged all my make-up.'

'You don't need it anyway.'

She glanced over at him reproachfully and then smiled. 'You haven't changed much,' she whispered. 'You're still incredibly…audacious.'

'And you're still incredibly hot. Do you remember that evening when we first started seeing each other? We were supposed to be going out to dinner and then the opera…but we didn't even make it through the main course.'

Gemma held the darkness of his eyes for a long moment. She remembered that evening well. The hurried speed with which Marcus had paid the bill, the way they had started to undress each other as soon as they had stepped through the front door of his house. She had often wondered if that was the night Liam had been conceived.

'Yes, I remember…' She whispered the words huskily and wanted to tell him that no one had ever held such compelling power over her senses, either before or since.

'They were good times,' Marcus said quietly.

The lightness of that remark brought her firmly to her right mind.

'Yes…' She looked away from him sharply. Of course she couldn't tell him how deeply he had touched her. It was far too revealing. Letting Marcus know that she was completely besotted by him would serve little purpose other than to feed his ego. And in the process it would leave her open and vulnerable.

But guarding her heart from her husband was not how Gemma had ever envisioned her wedding day.

She looked down at the gold wedding band on her finger. 'Can I ask you something?'

'Fire away.'

'When Liam was in hospital and you asked me to marry you…'

'Yes?'

'Was it a spur of the moment thing? You know… Were you so worried about Liam and about having to leave that the question just popped out?'

'No, it wasn't a spur of the moment thing.' He said the words firmly, then reached to touch her face so that she would look at him. 'I'd been giving the idea careful thought from the moment I realized I was leaving London. In fact, Liam must have heard me talking about it on the phone just before he was taken ill.'

'I thought you were planning to marry…someone else.' She couldn't even bring herself to say Sophia's name—not on her wedding day.

Marcus shook his head. 'Only you,' he said softly.

The words made her heart bounce crazily against her chest.

'I wanted to take you out to dinner to ask you properly, but you kept refusing to see me…then events were taken out of my hands when Liam became ill.'

'Out of the hands of both of us,' Gemma murmured.

Marcus nodded. His eyes were so cool and serious on her face that she felt them as if they were touching her. 'You've given up a lot to come here…your job, your friends…'

Some small spark of devilment made her say softly, 'Richard was devastated…'

'To hell with Richard.' Marcus's eyes narrowed on her face, and for a fraction of one joyous moment

Gemma wondered if he was jealous. If maybe, deep down, he really did love her…

'You belong to me now, Gemma.' He leaned forward and his lips touched hers with sizzling heat and passion.

It took a moment before either of them realized that the car had come to a standstill. They broke apart and, looking out, saw that they were outside a pretty country inn and that other cars were pulling up around them.

'I guess it's time to get the wedding show back on the road.' Marcus grinned over at her. 'But let's leave as soon as possible…hmm?' His eyes drifted down over her body. 'Because it's time I had you all to myself. Claimed what is rightfully mine.'

The words made her burn inside with desire and need.

CHAPTER NINE

THE setting for their wedding banquet was idyllic. The quaint whitewashed old inn backed out on to the most charming garden where long white-clothed trestle tables were laid up under the leafy shade of a vine-covered pergola.

A bar had been set up at the end of the lawn and for a while the guests mingled, chatting happily as they sipped *aperitivo* wine and ate small salted biscuits. A warm breeze stirred the cypress trees, lifting the intensity of the afternoon heat.

Gemma glanced across the lawn to where Liam was playing happily in the shade with his cousins. In the few days since they had arrived he had caught the sun and his skin was a golden brown. He looked the picture of health and it was hard to believe he was the same little boy who had been so pale and ill in the hospital.

Her gaze moved towards Marcus who was deep in conversation with his father and two of his brothers. The Rossini men were all handsome, but it was Marcus who drew her attention. She couldn't keep her eyes off him. As if sensing her gaze, he turned and looked over at her and smiled. She smiled back.

'And you tried to tell me you weren't in love with him,' her mother said in a teasingly low voice next to her and she felt herself blushing guiltily. 'He's very good-looking, isn't he?'

'Yes,' Gemma agreed. 'Too good-looking for any woman's peace of mind.'

'And I can see where he gets his looks from as well. Giorgio is a very attractive man.'

Gemma smiled and looked questioningly up at her mother. 'Oh, yes?'

Joanne shrugged and then to Gemma's surprise blushed a little. 'He's asked me to accompany him to the opera tomorrow night.'

Gemma remembered that similar invitation from Marcus and her eyes widened a little. 'Well, tread carefully, Mum. The Rossini men can be very charming.'

Joanne laughed. 'This is your old mum you are talking to! It's just dinner and the opera.'

'Less of the "old", you look fantastic,' Gemma said honestly. Her mother did look beautiful in a pale blue suit with a matching wide-brimmed hat.

Some other relatives of Marcus came over to speak to them and the conversation was forgotten. Then, a little while later, everyone took their places at the table.

Gemma sat next to Marcus at the head of the table and then Giorgio opposite to her mother with Liam beside her. In all there were about sixty people at the long table, and, with the exception of Jane and Steve they were all Marcus's family.

There was lots of laughter and the wine flowed with the many courses. The waiters brought out vast silver platters with canapés of smoked salmon and stuffed olives, tiger prawns, lobster. They circulated many times, first with the hot antipasto then the cold. After that they brought different types of pasta, Gemma's favourite being the restaurant's own delicious tagliatelle, and then the main course of aromatic lamb.

All through the meal guests were proposing toasts to the bride and groom. There was much teasing and laughing. Marcus watched how Gemma blushed when someone said that he hoped their union would be blessed with many, *many* children. Then someone else jumped up and said he hoped that their table would always groan under the weight of good food.

That made Gemma laugh. 'I can see I'm going to have to take up lessons in Italian cooking while I'm here,' she said jokingly to Marcus.

'What do you mean, *while* you are here?' He looked at her with a quizzical lift of one eyebrow. 'You're here to stay, Gemma, remember?'

Her heart missed a beat at those words. Then he leaned closer and whispered playfully against her ear. 'And don't worry, I'm a very modern man—I won't keep you barefoot and pregnant in the kitchen…just naked and ready for me in the bedroom.'

She knew he was only joking but there was something so riskily sexual about the vision he conjured up that she felt the heat of pure lust lick deep inside her. He laughed with delight as he saw the echo of that heat in the deep blue of her eyes.

A chant went around the table as suddenly everyone insisted that the groom should kiss his bride.

Marco grinned and leaned closer to oblige. The heat of his lips was seductively mesmerising against hers and as she kissed him back she wished fervently that they were on their own.

There were no stilted formal speeches but as the wedding cake was carried in to loud applause, Giorgio got to his feet to propose another toast. 'I just want to say how glad I am that you two have got together,' he said with deep sincerity in his eyes, 'and to propose a toast to members of the family who are not here. My late wife…Gemma's father…and of course Freddie, who introduced you two in the first place.' He smiled. 'It was a wonderful day when he brought you into our lives, Gemma.'

She smiled at her father-in-law, deeply touched by the words.

The light was starting to fade in the garden as the cake was cut and champagne was served. Fairy lights were turned on and they sparkled amongst the trees and along the trellis. The tables were swiftly cleared so that candles could be placed along the centre and a small band set up next to the bar area and played romantic Italian melodies.

As people got up to dance and mill about near the bar, more guests arrived and came over to congratulate them. For a little while she was separated from Marcus and it was Helene who introduced her to the late arrivals, most of whom were friends and neighbours of the family.

'And of course you met Sophia Albani at my wedding,' Helene said casually. Gemma turned and with a deep jolt found herself face to face with the woman who had haunted her thoughts for so long.

Sophia hadn't changed a bit. She was still arrestingly beautiful. A turquoise dress fitted tightly over the sensual curves of her body, dipping provocatively at the neckline and skimming her small waist and narrow hips. She had high cheekbones, almond shaped brown eyes and long glossy dark hair.

Although the woman smiled at her, her eyes were cold. 'I believe congratulations are in order.'

'Thank you.' Gemma had never felt more awkward in all her life. She didn't know what to say and she was astounded that the woman was even here. If their situations had been reversed, there was no way Gemma would have attended her marriage with Marcus. But maybe Sophia had moved on…maybe she was in love with someone else by now and didn't care?

'Sorry I didn't make it to the church today but I had another important engagement and I couldn't get out of it.' Sophia took a glass of champagne from the tray of a passing waiter.

'It was a beautiful service,' Helene said. 'Not a dry eye in the place.'

'Yes… I'm sure.' As Sophia lifted the glass to her lips Gemma noticed the sparkle of a wedding ring on her finger and the feeling of relief that swept through her was immense.

'I see you've got married since we last met?' Gemma said, wondering when this event had taken place.

'Yes, two months ago. Alberto is around here somewhere,' she said nonchalantly, her eyes searching the crowds. 'He's probably at the bar with the men.'

Helene turned away from them to talk to someone else and they were left momentarily alone.

'Well, Marcus and I decided it was for the best…' Sophia continued. 'We both had to get on with our lives.'

'Sorry?' Gemma was lost now.

Sophia smiled and there was something rather pitying in her expression. 'You know that Marcus and I have always…had an understanding? We're soul mates. Have been together from the junior school.'

Gemma wasn't sure how she should be handling this at all—or where it was leading. 'Well, Freddie told me that you used to…date Marcus, if that's what you mean.'

'It was a little more than that.' Sophia's eyes were hard now, like chips of granite. 'Until he went to England and got—how shall I put it…encumbered. Yes, encumbered with a child.'

'I don't think Marcus would put it like that. He adores Liam.' Gemma's voice was equally cold now and her heart was beating angrily in her chest.

'Yes, he does. You were very clever. Produced a son, then played to Marcus's sense of duty. It would have killed him to let go of Liam, so he had to propose, and you got him in the end.' Sophia lifted her glass in a mocking salute. 'I have to hand it to you, it was a very clever strategy. Shame he doesn't love you, though. How do you live with that? It must be awful knowing you've got him by default, and that I'm the woman he really wanted…'

'That is absolute rubbish.' Gemma's voice was very low now and very icy. 'Marcus adores me.' Even as she uttered the lie, Gemma wondered if a bolt of lightning would strike her.

'Does he?' Sophia smiled. 'So how come he spent his last night of freedom in my arms, telling me he wished things were different?'

With a small smile of satisfaction Sophia walked away from her.

'What's the matter?' Helene asked in consternation as she turned back towards Gemma and saw the sudden pallor of her skin.

'Nothing…it was just something Sophia said.'

'What did she say?' Helene asked sharply.

'Nothing.' Gemma shrugged, too embarrassed to tell the other woman the exact conversation. 'Just something about how her and Marcus were childhood sweethearts.'

'Oh, is that all?' Helene laughed. 'Marcus is a grown man now, Gemma. He put away his childhood toys a long time ago. He loves you—he married you. Pay no attention to Sophia. It is a case of…what's the English phrase…sour wine?'

'Sour wine?' Gemma was momentarily distracted. 'Oh, I think you mean sour grapes.'

'That's it!' Helene laughed.

And Gemma had to smile.

Helene put an arm around her shoulder. 'That's Sophia's husband over there.' She indicated a tall man with an ugly profile and balding head. 'Her papà helped her pick him out when it was decided Marcus was no longer…'available'. He's practically a millionaire and very well connected to help Sophia's father, business-wise. Plus he keeps Sophia in very good style, and as she has hardly ever worked a day in her life that suits her fine. But look at him! It's no wonder Sophia is a little bitter.'

Gemma shook her head. 'Maybe he is a lovely person, Helene,' she rebuked lightly.

'Well, maybe he is, and maybe they love each other deeply, but I doubt it somehow. I think their marriage is a business arrangement more than anything.'

Gemma couldn't say anything to that, because deep down she knew her marriage to Marcus was little more than a sham itself. He didn't love her, he was doing this for Liam, and all these people who had flocked to wish them well were just being taken in by an illusion… Everyone except for Sophia, of course.

The buoyant feeling of happiness that had been with her since walking into the chapel today suddenly disappeared completely. She had almost been taken in by the illusion herself. Marcus could play the adoring bridegroom to perfection.

She saw him making his way towards her through the crowds and her heart started to race nervously. Tonight he would want to take the illusion one step further and sleep with her. How was she going to deal with that, knowing for certain that he still loved Sophia?

He reached her side and smiled at her. 'Liam has found himself a girlfriend.'

Gemma glanced over to where her son was dancing hand in hand with Helene's four-year-old daughter, Andrea who looked very appealing in her long white frilly dress.

'Obviously he has inherited the Rossini charm,' she managed to reply with a smile.

'Obviously.' Marcus's gaze moved over her face. 'Shall we have a dance before we sneak away from the party?'

The question made apprehension rise even further inside her. 'Yes…' She nodded. 'Good idea, then we really should take Liam home. He must be exhausted.' Maybe she could delay the inevitable by staying with Liam in his room for a while, she thought desperately. Maybe she could even say that Liam didn't want her to leave him alone tonight…? She just wanted to buy some time to think about this situation.

'Liam is coming back to Papà's house with us, Gemma,' Helene said, glancing at her watch. 'We'll be rounding up all the children in a few minutes.'

This was the first Gemma had heard of such a plan. 'That's very kind of you, Helene,' she said quickly. 'But I wouldn't hear of it. You've got enough children staying at the house, plus you've got my guests.'

'There's plenty of room and there are plenty of adults around to help with the children. Liam is coming with us,' Helene said with equal firmness. 'This is your wedding night, Gemma. You and Marcus relax and enjoy yourselves. We will take care of Liam.'

Gemma wanted to argue further but Marcus took hold

of her hand. 'Come on, let's have that dance,' he said with a grin.

Marcus led her on to the small wooden dance floor and suddenly everyone started to applaud. Gemma was conscious of a sea of faces around them, watching as he pulled her closer into his arms.

'Relax.' He whispered the word against her ear as she held herself stiffly against him.

'Why?' She angled her head up to look at him and couldn't quite conceal the shimmering resentment in her voice. 'Because everyone is watching?'

'Because otherwise I might step on your toes.' He grinned. 'You are fighting against me…relax and go with the flow, let me lead.'

'And that's something you are very good at, isn't it Marcus?' she murmured dryly.

'Yes, it is.' He put a hand under her chin as she made to look away from him. 'What's the matter?'

'Nothing.' She jerked away from him and then, conscious that they were being watched, forced herself to smile at him. 'Nothing…' she said again in a softer tone. She didn't want to start a deep and angry conversation with him now. And anyway, what was the point?

Really, she had no right to be angry with him. She'd gone into this marriage with her eyes wide open. Marcus hadn't lied to her; he'd never said he loved her.

People had joined them on the dance floor now and she was forced to stay close to him in the tightly confined space.

He put an arm around her and held her close. She was conscious of the hard pressure of his body against hers, the delicious tang of his aftershave, the familiar warmth of his arms. She closed her eyes and leaned against his chest, giving herself up to the pleasure of just being held.

'That's better,' Marcus whispered. His voice tickled against her ear. 'Are you tired, my darling?'

The husky endearment made her squeeze her eyes tight against sudden tears. 'A little.'

'It's been a long day.'

'Yes.' She breathed in the scent of him, the delicious tenderness in his manner. She wanted so much to forget that their marriage was based purely on practicalities; she wanted to drown in his arms, accept the passion of his kisses and the heat of his body. The thought of the night ahead tempted her senses beyond endurance. She wanted desperately to shut out every negative and painful thought that was in her mind and just give in to the delights of being with him.

'Shall we go?'

The whispered question was accompanied by the touch of his lips against her neck. The sweet rush of pleasure was almost more than she could bear.

'Yes…' Her heart pounded heavily against her chest. 'I just want to say goodnight to Liam, make sure everything is all right with him.'

'Fine. I'll sneak out and get the car started. Meet you outside the front of the inn in, say, ten minutes?'

She nodded.

It sounded like a secret assignation—exciting, wonderfully clandestine. As she hurried away she pulled herself up. The only clandestine meeting that Marcus would look forward to was a meeting with Sophia.

Was she so pathetically in love that she would take any crumb of endearment? Where was her dignity, her pride now?

She spotted Liam sitting at the table with her mother and four of his cousins.

'Are you okay, darling?' She crouched down beside

him and he nodded happily. 'Do you want to come home with me now?' She knew everyone would be cross with her for taking him, but she didn't want to leave him.

Liam frowned. 'No, I'm going home with Nana and Auntie Helene and Andrea...oh, and Bruno is coming as well. We're going to have a midnight feast.'

'It's almost midnight now. Why don't you come home with Daddy and me?'

Liam shook his head. 'I don't want to. Grandad is going to take us to the zoo tomorrow and Bruno and Peter are coming too.' He indicated the two cousins that were nearest to him in age. 'And Nana is coming...' Liam added excitedly. 'I want to stay with them.'

Gemma's mother put a hand on her arm. 'Leave him, Gemma. You go with your husband now. I'll take care of Liam, I promise.'

Gemma nodded. 'Okay. Thanks, Mum. I'll see you tomorrow.'

Her mother smiled. 'Or the day after...' she added mischievously.

'I'll ring you in the morning,' Gemma said and gave Liam a kiss. 'Be good.'

Gemma headed away from the crowds of people and around the side of the inn. The gnarled shapes of olive and lemon trees were outlined against the bright starry sky. There was a smell of citrus blossom in the night air.

As the voices and the music faded away, all Gemma was left with was the sound of her heart beating heavily against her chest and the tropical sound of the cicadas.

She saw Marcus waiting for her, leaning against the bonnet of a car. He straightened as she walked over.

'Was Liam okay?'

She nodded.

'He'll enjoy being at Dad's house with all the other children.'

'I still think he should have come back with us.' Her voice was brusque. 'We are supposed to be keeping a close eye on him, remember?'

'Of course I remember.' Marcus opened the passenger door for her. 'It's the reason you married me, isn't it?'

There it was—the truth, awkward and painful but inescapable. 'Yes. It is.' She walked towards him to get into the car. 'And for that reason we should have brought him home with us tonight. We're a family, not a couple. We may have to pretend for everyone else's sake that we are madly in love, but at least we can be honest with each other.'

'I thought we were being honest.' Marcus's voice was hard and cutting.

She paused next to him and looked up into his eyes. She wished she could see the expression on his face but it was in shadow. She took a deep breath and launched in before she could change her mind. 'So I really think the decent thing would be for us to sleep in separate rooms.'

There was a moment's silence.

'You don't mean that?'

The arrogance of that remark made her angle her head up defiantly. 'Yes, I do.'

'We have an arrangement, Gemma. You are my wife and tonight we *will* consummate the marriage.'

She opened her mouth to say something further and then closed it again. The ominous dark tones of his voice were not to be argued with. And she supposed he was right, she had made an agreement with him.

'Get in the car.' His voice was softer now. 'We'll talk about this when we get home.'

She did as he asked. Her heart was pumping so heavily in her chest it felt like it might explode.

CHAPTER TEN

IT WAS a short drive along narrow twisting roads towards Marcus's villa. Neither of them spoke along the way and Gemma tried not to think too deeply about the rights and wrongs of what lay ahead.

The truth was she wanted to sleep with Marcus so badly it hurt. And she wished now that she hadn't said anything to him. It was pride that had made her sound off…stupid and misplaced pride. She had already married him. There was no going back. They could only go forward. And the thought of lying in a separate room from him tonight was not agreeable. Where could their marriage go from there? And she wanted this marriage to work…wanted it with all her heart.

The road ahead glinted gold in the lights of the powerful headlights and the landscape around them was bathed in a strange silver light from the full moon. But Gemma hardly noticed anything. All she could think about was the situation she found herself in.

Maybe Marcus wouldn't see Sophia again; she said the words to herself fiercely. Maybe last night had been their final farewell? The notion wasn't even slightly reassuring. In fact, it just smacked of hopelessness.

Marcus turned the car through high gateposts and down a gravel drive lined with sentinel pine trees. A few minutes later she could see the outline of his house silhouetted against the night sky: a huge rambling farmhouse, flanked at each side by majestic black cypresses.

'Home, sweet home.' Marcus's voice was dry.

She didn't answer him.

He brought the car to a standstill by the front door and then climbed out without a word.

Gemma followed him, lifting her long dress to walk up the steps towards the front door.

The silence of the countryside added to Gemma's feeling of unease. She was used to the rumble of traffic night and day in the city. The sounds here were of insects and the rustle of creatures in the hedgerows.

As Marcus put his key in the latch, Gemma looked out over the meadows beside them and noticed pinpoints of flickering, pulsating light. 'What's that?' she asked, putting a hand on his shoulder.

Marcus followed her gaze out across the fields. 'Fireflies.' He looked back at her, momentary amusement in his eyes. 'They won't bite. The only thing that bites around here is me.'

'Very funny.'

The door swung open but before she could precede him into the darkened hallway, Marcus put his arm around her waist and swung her easily up off her feet and into his arms.

'Put me down!' The action took her by surprise and her arms went instinctively up around his neck.

He ignored the request. 'No, I won't put you down, Mrs Rossini.' He smiled, his eyes lingering on her lips. 'I'm observing custom and carrying you over the threshold.'

She wondered if he was going to kiss her. She wanted him to. In fact, she would have liked him to carry her in and straight up the stairs to the marital bed. She was ashamed of herself for such weakness but she couldn't help it.

However, Marcus didn't kiss her and as soon as they

were inside the house he did put her down and then flicked on the hall lights.

She busied herself smoothing down the soft silk of her long skirt. Now that they were under the glare of bright lights she didn't want him to look at her too closely in case she gave herself away…in case he read the desire in her eyes.

'Shall we have a drink?' He moved away from her towards the lounge.

She followed him, glancing curiously around the impressive hallway, with its wide staircase and galleried landing. Marcus had invited her up to the villa a couple of days ago, but she had snatched the excuse of a shopping trip with Helene in Rome instead. She supposed she had been putting off the inevitable, even then.

What exactly was she scared of? she wondered as she watched him pouring whisky into a crystal tumbler.

He glanced over and the darkness of his eyes seemed to slice through her. 'Do you want to join me or are you going to go upstairs to make yourself more comfortable?'

The question brought a blaze of heat to her skin.

'I'll have a drink, thanks.' She moved further into the lounge from the doorway.

Gemma didn't drink whisky, but it was preferable to going upstairs to make herself more 'comfortable'. What did he expect her to do? Go up to the bedroom and take all her clothes off and wait for him?

She accepted the glass from him with a slightly shaking hand and their skin touched accidentally. The sharp feeling of yearning that ran through her at the contact was shocking in its intensity. And suddenly she knew exactly what she was afraid of. *Losing control.* Allowing him to find out just how much she still wanted him...throwing away all the carefully constructed barriers of pride that she had built up around herself over the years.

Once he touched her she was lost and she knew it. *He probably knew it as well.* Hadn't he demonstrated it to her the last time they were alone in her bedroom in London?

Marcus touched his glass against hers in a salute. 'Alone at last,' he murmured sardonically.

Something about the toast reminded her of Sophia's mocking salute earlier. 'Well, you don't have to be alone with me,' she said flippantly. 'The ink is still wet on the marriage certificate—we could probably get it annulled.'

'For non-consummation?'

'Why not?' She shrugged lightly. 'Maybe this marriage was a crazy idea to begin with.'

'Maybe it was.' Marcus regarded her through a narrowed glittering dark gaze. 'But we've already been through the marriage ceremony, so as far as I'm concerned, it's a bit late for cold feet. We made an agreement, Gemma...' As he spoke he was unfastening the silk cravat at his neck.

There was something very purposeful about the move.

Gemma took a sip of her whisky; it burnt the back of her throat and made her cough. She turned away from him nervously, pretended to be looking around the room.

A huge fireplace dominated one wall; it was raised off the floor on a flagstone platform and the stone chimney breast soared to the high ceiling. The furniture was in keeping with the rustic charm of the place; comfortable chairs and a settee in a pale buttermilk colour.

'Well, if I'm going to stay, then I suppose you should show me around the house,' she murmured, trying to turn the subject away from the sleeping arrangements.

There were some photographs sitting on a side table and she picked one of them up absently, noticing that it was the same photograph that she had looked at long ago at Marcus's London house—Marcus as a young teenager with his younger brothers. Her eyes lingered on it for a moment, remembering that night when she had gone to interview Marcus. Remembering how much she had wanted him from that first moment.

Marcus came across and took the photograph away from her to put it face down on the polished surface. 'What's all this really about, Gemma?' he grated harshly. 'You were quite happy to go along with our arrangement this morning…what's changed?'

Gemma didn't answer him immediately. She supposed nothing had changed. She had known when she walked down the aisle that morning that Marcus didn't love her. She had just foolishly tried to convince herself for a few hours that he did. And if Sophia hadn't broken the illusion so brutally she would probably be still fooling herself now…but that was her fault, not Marcus's.

Suddenly she remembered Freddie telling her how he'd come over here on the morning before Helene's wedding to deliver some flowers and had found Marcus and Sophia *in flagrante*.

What was it Freddie had said… *'Those two can't keep their hands off each other.'*

She looked up at him with shimmering blue eyes. 'Nothing has changed,' she whispered unsteadily. 'I suppose you are right and I've just got cold feet…plus I'm a bit tired.'

Marcus frowned. Then he reached out and took the crystal glass from her hand. 'Come on, I'll show you upstairs,' he said softly.

As she followed him out towards the hallway her heart

started to beat with an uneven and nervous tattoo against her chest again.

'The kitchen is over there.' Marcus waved towards a doorway at the other side of the hall. 'And there is a study and a smaller morning room at the back of the house.'

She tried to concentrate on the practical tone of his voice and not on the fact that she was now following him upstairs.

'There are seven bedrooms.' Marcus reached and opened one of the doors. 'This one is for Liam.'

She stepped inside the doorway and looked around. The room was beautifully decorated in pale blue. All Liam's toys were waiting for him, lined up along the shelves. Marcus had obviously given the room a lot of time and thought. His thoughtfulness and his love for his child never failed to move Gemma.

'It's lovely,' she whispered.

He turned away and opened the door next to it. 'And this is our room.'

She stepped into the large bedroom and glanced around at the tasteful décor, the pale cream carpets, the fitted wardrobes, before her eyes lingered on the enormous double bed.

'It's all right, don't look so worried. I've never forced a woman to sleep with me in my life and I don't intend to start now.'

He waved a hand towards another door at the end of the room. 'There's a bathroom through there. And you'll find your clothes in the far wardrobes. My housekeeper should have unpacked most of your stuff.'

'Where are you going?' she asked shakily as she watched him gather up a few of his belongings.

'I'll be next door. If you change your mind and want

to share my bed then just come on through.' He closed the door firmly behind him on the way out.

She sat down on the edge of the bed and glared at the door. Who the hell did he think he was? she thought angrily. *'If you change your mind just come through,'* indeed! If he was the last man left in the universe she wouldn't follow him through there now, not after that arrogant exit.

Gemma caught sight of her reflection in the dressing table mirror opposite. She was extremely pale; her eyes seemed to dominate her small face and her wedding dress looked ghostly and unreal.

Was she going to let Sophia sabotage her marriage before it had even started?

The question ricocheted through her mind. If she let Marcus sleep in another room wasn't it tantamount to handing him to the other woman on a plate?

She stood up from the bed. She didn't give a toss, she told herself fiercely. Sophia was welcome to him.

With trembling fingers she undid the top seed pearl buttons on her dress. Then she realized that she couldn't reach the other buttons down the back of the dress.

She stretched and stretched, but to no avail. Sitting back down on the bed she tried to think what she should do. It was either sleep in her wedding dress or go next door and ask Marcus to take her out of it and she knew very well what he would make of that.

She kicked off her shoes and lay back against the pillows. To hell with it, she'd sleep like this.

But sleep refused to come. Her mind seemed to be racing in a million different directions. Gemma glared up at the ceiling. Then, in an agony of anger and frustration, she jumped up and went out into the hallway to march into the bedroom next door.

Marcus was coming out of the en-suite bathroom with just a towel around his waist. His hair was wet and his bronzed skin still glistened with water. He grinned at her and didn't seem to be the slightest bit surprised to see her.

'It's not what you think,' she said quickly. 'I just want you to get me out of this dress.'

'Really?' One dark eyebrow rose mockingly. 'I've had some invitations from women in my time, but never one quite so blunt.'

'I don't mean I want you to sleep with me.' She tried to make her eyes stay on his face but they kept drifting down to his body. He had an incredible physique—powerful shoulders and chest tapering down to a flat stomach and narrow hips. 'Just unbutton my dress, please.'

'Come here, then.'

The quiet command made her senses jump with nervous anticipation. She walked over towards him and then turned around so that he could see the buttons.

The touch of his hands against her made her heart thump loudly. Deftly he unfastened them down to her waist. Then, before she could move away, he slipped his hand in against her bare skin and pulled her back against him. She could feel the hairs on his chest, damp against her skin. 'I think that deserves a kiss, don't you?' he whispered playfully against her ear.

He kissed the side of her neck and as he did so he slowly pulled the dress down.

Gemma couldn't move, she just stood there transfixed by the sensation of pleasure as his lips trailed heatedly over her shoulders. As his fingers brushed over the curves of her breast she felt weak with longing for him.

She was wearing a lacy strapless bra beneath the dress, and it held the contours of her curves in a very provocative way. One more pull of the dress and the silk slid to the floor, revealing the lacy panties and the hold-up stockings that shimmered glossily on long shapely legs.

'There, that's better.' Marcus turned her to face him then and regarded her with a cool appraisal. Then he reached out and stroked one finger slowly and deliberately over the lace bra. Her nipples were so erect that he could feel them pushing against his hand. There was a gleam of triumph in his eyes as they moved upwards to hold with hers.

'You see, Gemma? Sexually, you want me very much…'

She shook her head, defiance shimmering in her blue eyes, and he thought he had never seen any woman so beautiful in all his life.

'You're a really bad liar, Gemma.' As he spoke he was lowering his head towards hers. Then his lips captured hers in a fiercely provocative and invasive kiss that sent all her senses reeling. After a few seconds she kissed him back with equal fervour—she couldn't stop herself. Her mind was saying one thing but her body was saying another in much more persuasive terms.

'You see? We've always been sexually compatible.' His tone was arrogantly assertive, but she didn't care. He pulled her closer and she wound her arms up and around his neck, standing on tiptoe to kiss him back heatedly.

She wanted him so much it was like an all-consuming fire inside her. And she was melting fast.

Then abruptly he stepped back and placed one hand under her chin, forcing her to keep eye contact. 'Say "please, Marcus make love to me".'

She stared at him mutinously and he smiled. 'I've

never met anyone as stubborn in all my life as you...Gemma Rossini.'

'Why are you playing these games?' Her voice sounded very distorted, not at all like her.

'I'm not the one playing games, Gemma, you are,' he said calmly. 'You pretend all the time. You pretended with Freddie...and probably with Richard too. And with me.'

'What are you talking about?' She was mystified.

'I'm talking about the way you like to tease men. I've seen you in action, Gemma, you are really very good.' He reached out and touched her, smoothed a stray strand of her hair back from her face. 'But it stops here...' he murmured softly. 'Because you belong to me now and there will be no more games...no more pretending...' He reached behind her and unfastened her bra.

'Now repeat after me...''please, Marcus, make love to me''.' As he spoke he was caressing the fullness of her breasts with both his hands, his thumbs running over her erect nipples with practised skill, making her catch her breath with a gasp of need.

Then his hands moved to the panties, pulling them down roughly and then stroking between her legs.

She was so aroused now that she was past thinking about anything other than the need to have him possess her completely.

'Please Marcus...' She moved into his arms willingly. 'Please make love to me.'

He pushed her down on to the softness of the bed and then, taking the towel from around his waist, he joined her.

Pinning her to the mattress with his body he slowly kissed her all over—her neck, her shoulders, then lower towards her breasts, taking his time pleasuring her so

much that she felt impatient with longing. She just
wanted to feel him inside her.

She had forgotten how wonderful his body felt against
hers, how he knew exactly where to touch her, what to
do to heighten her pleasure completely. As they clung
wildly to each other, kissing and touching, Gemma was
lost in a spiralling frenzy of pure desire.

When at last she felt his body inside hers she gasped
with pure pleasure.

She writhed against him, her hands raking over his
back.

'That's so good,' she cried out as he thrust even
deeper within her.

'You belong to me, Gemma Rossini.' He ground the
words fiercely as he penetrated her deeper and deeper,
holding her head with his hands and then plundering her
mouth with his tongue. 'Never…ever…forget that…'

Each word was punctuated by an extra push, and she
felt the world suddenly spinning off its axis into a blur
of complete and utter ecstasy.

Gemma stretched languidly in the bed. She felt unusu-
ally stiff and achy. She opened her eyes and looked
around the unfamiliar room. Sunlight was filtering
through the curtains, playing over the pretty lilac wallpaper and the bowl of roses on the dresser. There was a
sound of a bird singing outside the window, but nothing
else, no hint of human movement, no roar of traffic.

For a moment she was so disoriented that she couldn't
remember where she was. Then as she sat up, she saw
the crumpled heap of her wedding dress on the floor and
the events of the night before came rushing back like
the roar of the incoming tide.

Quickly she glanced over to the other side of the bed.

But it was empty. Memories from the night before trickled hotly through her mind. It was no wonder she was tired. The night had been filled with the heated passion of their lovemaking. Three, maybe four times, Marcus had possessed her. Then in the early hours of the morning he had woken her to take her again. It had been wild and tempestuous…and it was no wonder that her body felt tenderly dazed. She lay back against the pillows, drinking in the memories for a while. Lovemaking with Marcus was fabulous. She remembered now why no other man had ever come close to arousing her like he did. Just thinking about it made her body throb with need again.

Impatiently she pushed back the covers and walked towards the bathroom to have a shower. Standing under the heavy jet of water, she wondered where Marcus was. Wherever he was, she wanted him to come back so that they could continue where they had left off.

She smiled to herself, snapped the water off and reached blindly for a towel. To her surprise, one was placed in her hand. She looked up and saw Marcus standing outside the shower, fully dressed in jeans and a white shirt.

'Morning.' He smiled at her and his eyes raked boldly down over the naked curves of her body.

'Morning.' She grabbed the towel and wrapped it around her. It was ridiculous but suddenly she felt very shy. 'What time is it?'

'Seven-thirty.' He stepped back to allow her out of the shower. 'I thought we might go for an early morning ride.'

'Sounds fun.' She smiled. 'But I'm not very good at riding. You'll have to find me a reliable mount.'

'Oh, I think I can do that all right.' His eyes gleamed with teasing good humour and she felt herself blush.

He reached and pulled her towards him and then kissed her fully on the lips in a sensually provocative way.

The towel slipped to the floor as she reached to wind her arms around his neck.

She felt his hands moving over her possessively, holding her and touching her with arrogant ease. 'See you outside in a little while, okay?' He pulled back from her.

'Okay…' She watched him walk away from her, aware that she was a little disappointed because she had wanted him all over again.

She picked up the towel and hurriedly dried herself, then walked back to the bedroom to find something to put on, before remembering her clothes were in the bedroom next door.

It was half an hour before Gemma went downstairs, dressed in fawn cropped trousers and matching T-shirt. Her hair swung silkily around her shoulders and she had a bounce in her step. She was married to Marcus… The words sang happily in her mind. Maybe he hadn't told her he loved her but he sure as hell had *made love* to her. And suddenly that was enough for now.

She stepped into the kitchen, a high square room with a red tiled floor and beamed ceiling. There was a state-of-the-art cooker and light oak cupboards and also another massive fireplace like the one in the lounge. The house really had a lot of charm, Gemma thought as she opened the fridge and poured herself a glass of fresh orange juice. Moving to open up the back door, she breathed in the scent of the early morning air. It was tinged with camomile and the peppery scent of rosemary from a small herb garden that ran down from the enclosed courtyard towards the orchard below.

Liam was going to love it here, she thought looking at all the open space for him to run and play. Marcus was right; this was a lovely place to bring up a child.

The phone rang and, afraid it might be her mother ringing because Liam was missing her, she went through to the hall to pick it up.

'Rossini residence,' she said with a smile.

'Hi, Gemma, it's Sophia. Will you put Marcus on the phone? I need to speak to him.'

'He isn't here,' Gemma said tersely. She had no intention of fetching Marcus to the phone for her.

'Left you already, has he?' The smirk in Sophia's tone dripped venom.

'Actually, he's waiting to take me out for an early morning ride. In case it has escaped your notice, we are on our honeymoon, and we are very much in love, so please go away and don't ring here again.' With a feeling of satisfaction she slammed the phone down. 'Put that in your pipe and smoke it,' she said, dusting her hands against her hips.

'Who were you talking to?' Marcus stepped out from the kitchen making her jump.

'Nobody.' She whirled around, frightened in case he had heard what she had just said.

He frowned. 'It's a bit early to be ringing anyone.'

'Well, that's okay, because they were ringing me.'

The phone rang again loudly in the silence of the house and Gemma's nerves jangled alarmingly. As Marcus reached to pick it up she put a detaining hand on his arm. 'Leave it,' she said gently. She didn't want him talking to Sophia...and she certainly didn't want

Sophia repeating what she had just said. 'It will be a wrong number again.'

She saw the look of disbelief in his eyes.

'Okay, it'll be Richard again.' She pulled at his arm. 'Let's get out into the sunshine and ignore it.'

To her relief the phone stopped ringing.

'Richard?' Marcus looked at her dryly. 'What the hell did he want at this hour?'

'He'd forgotten there was a time difference...' Gemma turned away from him towards the kitchen. 'He just wanted to tell me who got the job as editor...you know, at *Modern Times*.'

'If you wanted to know who got the job at *Modern Times* why didn't you just ask me?' Marcus glared at her.

'I didn't want to know, that's just what I told Richard.' Gemma whirled around to look at him, one hand on her hip. She hated lying, she was dreadful at it and she could feel her temperature rising phenomenally. Why hadn't she just been truthful and told him it was Sophia? Why was she tying herself in knots? 'Now, are we going for that ride or not?'

Marcus looked at her with dark cynical eyes. 'Yes, let's go.'

CHAPTER ELEVEN

THE Italian countryside was spectacularly beautiful, Gemma thought as they rode silently side by side. The only sound was the soft thud of the horses' hooves on the grass and the occasional snort from Marcus's black stallion, Rufus, who was straining at the reins impatiently, wanting his head. He was a magnificent animal, Gemma thought, noting how his coat gleamed blue-black in the sunshine and his black tail swished from side to side.

Obviously, Marcus was an accomplished rider to be able to handle such a beast. And he looked pretty magnificent himself, she thought wryly flicking a glance up at him.

'You okay?' Marcus met her eyes and she nodded.

'Do want to walk for a bit?'

'Will Rufus allow that?' Gemma asked with a smile. 'He looks like he wants to gallop off.'

'He'll have to be patient,' Marcus said with a grin, stroking the animal's neck.

'Okay, we'll walk for a bit,' Gemma said, quite glad to be able to get down from her horse.

The gentle roan that Marcus had picked out for her was perfect but she was still feeling a little stiff from the activities of the night before. Just thinking about last night set up another ache inside her, but this time it was the dull ache of longing.

Marcus dismounted and then reached to help her. She slid down and for a second was held in his arms.

Instantly her body responded to the intimacy, her senses flaring with heat. Shyly she stepped away from him. It was embarrassing the way she responded to him. She wondered if he found it amusing, or if it merely fed his ego?

She slanted a glance up at him to see if he had noticed, but he seemed deep in thought.

Gemma glanced out over the fields. It was almost high summer and the corn was nearly ripe—it glinted gold in the sun, interspersed with the scarlet of poppies and blue of cornflowers. The sky had the same incandescent blue of the cornflowers and the hills in the distance looked hazily purple. There was not a house or a person in sight.

'London seems like a long, long way away,' Gemma murmured, breathing in the warmth of the air.

'Missing it already?' Marcus asked wryly.

'No, of course not.'

'So why were you ringing Richard this morning?'

'I didn't.' Gemma's face flared red. 'I told you, he phoned me.'

'Just to tell you who got the job at your old office?'

'Yes…'

'So who did he say had got it?'

'Well…he didn't.' She wondered if her face was scarlet now. 'I told you, I said I didn't want to know.'

'Really.' Marcus's tone was dry. 'Was that because you are so upset at not having it yourself?'

'No, it's not.' She shook her head. 'I don't have any regrets at giving up that job, Marcus.' She looked over at him, her eyes clear and candid now. 'Liam has to come first for a while.'

'But I take it Richard doesn't understand that?'

She frowned. 'Yes, Richard understands… And while we are on the subject, what were you talking about last night when you accused me of leading Richard on?' She remembered the conversation suddenly. 'You said something about my leading Freddie on as well. That's absolute rubbish.'

'Is it?' Marcus looked over at her with frank disbelief in his eyes.

'Yes, it is.' Gemma stopped walking and turned to face him.

'Gemma, you should remember that I'm not as easy to dupe as Freddie.'

The sardonic tone made her frown. 'What the hell do you mean by that?'

'You know what I'm talking about.' Marcus shook his head. 'Freddie really believed you loved him, you know...thought you were saving yourself for marriage with him.'

Gemma's eyes widened. 'No, he didn't!'

'Drop the innocent act, Gemma, it won't wash with me,' Marcus said grimly. 'You strung Freddie along, promising him you'd sleep with him eventually. He told me all about it just before Helene's wedding.'

Gemma felt her face flare with furious colour. 'I didn't lead Freddie on in any way,' she said, her voice rising sharply. 'Why the hell would I have done that?'

'Because it was your way of getting what you wanted. By refusing to sleep with Freddie you got a proposal of marriage...by sleeping with me you got the job you were after. That was the way you operated.'

Gemma's mouth fell open in horror. 'You really think I'm that conniving?'

'I think you were once, yes, but not now. Having Liam seems to have changed you. You're warm and caring and you're a wonderfully good mother and—'

'Don't you dare patronize me,' Gemma snapped

fiercely and the horses beside her fidgeted nervously. 'I never once led Freddie on. He always knew exactly where he stood with me.'

'So why did you agree to go to Helene's wedding with him?'

'Because he said he'd get me the interview with you if I agreed to accompany him to Italy.' She waved aside his words as he started to speak. 'And I made it very clear that there were no strings attached and that I was just a friend. In fact I made it clear to the whole house when I arrived. Told your father in no uncertain terms when he made a remark linking us together…you should ask him.' Gemma glared at Marcus furiously, her eyes snapping like jewels in the pallor of her face. She took a deep breath. 'And, as for not sleeping with Freddie because I wanted him to propose, that is utterly preposterous. For a start, Freddie had already proposed to me six months earlier, and I turned him down.'

Marcus frowned. 'So why was he so shocked when I told him I was seeing you?'

'You told Freddie…?' For a second Gemma was side-tracked. 'When did you tell him?'

'I went straight to see him after you told me you were attending my sister's wedding with him. I wanted to know what was going on.'

'There was nothing going on!' Gemma glared at him.

'Yes, well, at that point I needed to hear that from him.' Marcus raked a hand through the darkness of his hair. 'You can imagine my horror when Freddie practically broke down. He was inconsolable…told me you were the woman he was planning to marry. That you were both deeply in love…'

Gemma was so shocked by this that she could hardly

speak. 'That's just not true! Freddie and I were never anything but friends. Why did he say that?'

There was a long moment of silence.

'I can understand him being shocked when you told him you were seeing me,' she continued, trying to go over the past carefully in her mind. 'You see, I could never bring myself to tell him about us. I should have done, right from the beginning. But…' She frowned. 'I guess I was frightened of hurting him. He had tried to get me into bed in the past and I'd always turned him down…how could I tell him that at the first meeting with his brother I fell…into bed.'

Her voice trembled a little, as she nearly said, *fell in love*. 'I remember when I came home after spending that first night with you, there was a message on my answering machine from Freddie asking me how I'd got on with the interview. I rang him back intending to tell him honestly, and then backed away from the subject. I thought if I left it a while, told him things had developed more slowly between us, that it might soften the blow.'

'So you never told Freddie you loved him?'

'No!' Gemma's voice was emphatic. She raked a hand through her hair in confusion. 'What I don't understand is, why did Freddie pretend he knew nothing about our affair when quite clearly he did. Are you sure you told him *before* Helene's wedding?'

'Of course I am. The conversation is etched in my mind for all time.'

'Yet he never said one word to me in Italy about knowing. And when I finally did tell him, after we returned to London, he acted so shocked…'

'Was that the night you told him you were pregnant with my child?'

Gemma nodded.

'Well, that's why he was shocked.' Marcus's voice grated derisively.

'Don't look at me like that, Marcus. I never led Freddie on in any way.'

'You were dancing pretty close to him at Helene's wedding.'

'He was comforting me because you were with Sophia. It was a bit of a shock finding out you were going to marry someone else, Marcus. Freddie told me all about it—how you two couldn't keep your hands off each other, how he'd gone around to the house to deliver flowers that very morning and caught you making love with her in the lounge—'

'He did what?' Marcus looked furious now.

'Look, there is no point being angry with Freddie for telling me that. I needed to know.'

'No, you didn't, because what he told you was a pack of lies.'

Gemma frowned sceptically. 'So there was never any question of you marrying Sophia?'

'There was an understanding once between our two families that Sophia and I would get married. But we were very young then, and it never worked out between us. Freddie knew that.'

'Yeah, right, and that was why you were making love to her in the lounge before Helene's wedding...'

'Freddie was lying, Gemma. There were no flowers that morning at my house, and no Sophia. The only thing that happened that morning was a last and terrible argument between my brother and I about you.'

Gemma stared at him for a few moments, her breath rising and falling heavily in her chest, and then she turned away from him. 'I don't believe you.'

'Think about it, Gemma,' Marcus called after her as

she walked away. 'If Freddie lied to me about how serious his relationship was with you…couldn't he also have lied to you?'

Gemma stopped walking.

'It seems to me that he was playing us off against each other, hoping you'd turn to him for comfort. It might have worked, as well, except for the fact that you were pregnant with my child.'

Gemma let go of the horse's reins and turned back towards him.

'And what about Sophia? Was she lying too?' Her voice was very unsteady now. 'Did she lie when she told me how much you loved her?'

'When the hell did she say that?' Marcus also let go of his horse to walk towards her. 'Things were over romantically between Sophia and I long before I left Italy.'

Gemma shook her head. 'I don't believe you. Because, according to Sophia you've always been in love with her. She used to visit you in London all the time.'

'That's not true, Gemma.' He grasped hold of her, bringing her tightly in against him. 'Yes, she called to see me a few times in London. But she didn't stay with me; she was over visiting other friends. She used to call around with gifts for Liam, she's very fond of him.'

Gemma looked at him sceptically.

'Sophia is like a part of my family, Gemma. She's always been around, but I swear there is nothing between us. There's been no one else in my life since the day I met you.'

Gemma swallowed hard, wanting so much to believe that.

'So where were you the night before our wedding, Marcus?' she asked him suddenly. 'How did you spend your last night of freedom?'

Marcus frowned. 'You know what I did. I came down to see you and Liam.'

'That was just for an hour. What did you do after that?'

'I went home.'

'According to Sophia, you were with her. Telling her how much you wished it was her and not me that you were marrying—' The look of astonishment on Marcus's face made her stop abruptly.

'That's not true, Gemma.' He caught her face in his hands earnestly. 'You've got to believe me. Sophia and I finished years ago…and I don't know why she is saying these things, but we will find out.' His voice shook with such fierce anger that suddenly Gemma could do nothing else but believe him.

'I love you.' He said the words with such emphatic fierceness that she felt her body shake with the force of his emotion. 'I'm crazy about you…always have been and always will be.'

'But…?' Gemma was looking up at him in wonder. 'You kept away from me for so long…even after Liam was born…'

'Because I was a fool.' He shook his head. 'I believed my brother…and every time I looked at you I was filled with remorse and guilt for what I'd done. I broke my brother's heart, Gemma. He died because of me, because of us…'

'No!' Gemma's eyes filled with tears of horror. 'That's not true, Marcus. It wasn't anybody's fault. He was driving too fast—you know what he was like, how careless he could be…' She reached up and stroked the side of his face with tender concern. 'It wasn't your fault…or mine.'

Marcus took a deep breath. 'I realize that now…

but…God, I miss him Gemma, he was my kid brother.'

'I know.' She reached up and suddenly they were in each other's arms, holding each other tight.

Then suddenly their embrace changed, turned from empathy and fierce emotion to a different kind of intensity. Gemma turned her head and found his lips and they kissed, a passionately sweet and searing kiss.

'Oh Marcus…' She raised herself up to hug him closer. 'I want you so much.'

She felt his hands on her body and suddenly it was as if they couldn't get enough of each other. He took hold of her hand and pulled her into the field of corn beside them, laying her down and kissing her again, his other hand pulling at her T-shirt.

Then they were naked in each other's arms, kissing each other, holding each other. Above her, Gemma could see the blue of the sky and the gold of the corn and she felt as if her life had never been so perfectly complete.

'I love you so much, Marcus,' she whispered the words huskily against his skin as she pulled him closer.

'What did you say?'

He pulled back and looked down at her.

'I love you…'

He smiled and leaned down to kiss her. 'God, you don't know how much I've longed to hear you say those words.' The relief in his voice was so deep it was palpable. 'I was frightened that you were starting to have feelings for Richard.'

Gemma shook her head. 'No. I'm fond of him, but…that was as deep as it went.'

'Really?' He held her head between his hands and looked deep into her eyes.

'Yes, really.'

'When I saw you together...' He paused. 'Hell, Gemma I was so jealous. It was as if a mist had lifted, leaving a clear vision of life without you, and I suddenly realized that it didn't matter about the past, all that mattered was the future, and I couldn't bear to lose you. I knew then that I had to get you back.'

Gemma stroked her hands along the sides of his face, tracing the contours of his features lightly. 'Richard is a nice guy but—'

'I don't care how nice he is.' He interrupted her firmly. 'No more phone calls from him first thing in the morning, okay?'

She winced. 'I've got a confession to make. That wasn't Richard this morning, it was Sophia.'

'What the hell did she want?'

'You, I suppose.'

'So why did you lie?' He stroked her hair back from her face. 'You should have told me. I don't know what her problem is, but I'd have dealt with her.'

'I didn't tell you because I didn't want you to know what I said to her.'

'What did you say?'

'That we loved each other and she should go away and leave us alone.'

Marcus laughed at that and pulled her closer, rolling over so that she was lying on top of him. 'I couldn't have put it better myself,' he said softly, then threaded his fingers through the gold of her hair and pulled her down to meet the passion of his lips.

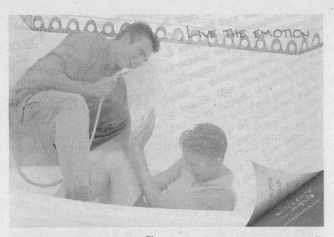

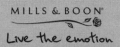

MILLS & BOON®

Live the emotion

Modern Romance™

THE MARRIED MISTRESS by Kate Walker

When the paparazzi get a tip-off about Greek tycoon Damon Nicolaides' new mistress they come flocking to her door. Actually, Sarah and Damon were secretly married a year ago, but Sarah left, thinking their marriage was a lie. Now Damon has come to claim the wife he truly loves...

IN THE BILLIONAIRE'S BED by Sara Wood

Catherine couldn't believe the Manor had been left to such a money-orientated workaholic as Zach Talent! But when she helped him bond with his small son she realised there was a good man underneath the prickly shell. However Zach had decided they were just too different to find lasting happiness...

TANGLED EMOTIONS by Catherine George

Fen Dysart has lost everything. But when she meets Joe Tregenna their passionate relationship almost makes her forget. Until Fen's world comes crashing down again, when Joe discovers the truth about her secret past and she learns that Joe hasn't been exactly honest either. It should be all over – but Joe can't get her out of his mind...

THE FRENCH COUNT'S MISTRESS by Susan Stephens

When Kate Foster decides to open a business deep in the French countryside, she imagines a return to the idyll of her childhood holidays. Instead she discovers that all the other properties on the impressive estate have been sold to none other than the sophisticated Count Guy de Villeneuve, on whom she once had a crush...

On sale 1st August 2003

Available at most branches of WH Smith, Tesco, Martins, Borders, Eason, Sainsbury's and all good paperback bookshops.

0703/01b

MILLS & BOON

STEPHANIE LAURENS

A Season for Marriage

Available from 18th July 2003

*Available at most branches of WH Smith,
Tesco, Martins, Borders, Eason, Sainsbury's
and all good paperback bookshops.*

0703/135/MB67

4 FREE

books and a surprise gift!

We would like to take this opportunity to thank you for reading this Mills & Boon® book by offering you the chance to take FOUR more specially selected titles from the Modern Romance™ series absolutely FREE! We're also making this offer to introduce you to the benefits of the Reader Service™—

- ★ FREE home delivery
- ★ FREE gifts and competitions
- ★ FREE monthly Newsletter
- ★ Exclusive Reader Service discount
- ★ Books available before they're in the shops

Accepting these FREE books and gift places you under no obligation to buy, you may cancel at any time, even after receiving your free shipment. Simply complete your details below and return the entire page to the address below. *You don't even need a stamp!*

YES! Please send me 4 free Modern Romance books and a surprise gift. I understand that unless you hear from me, I will receive 6 superb new titles every month for just £2.60 each, postage and packing free. I am under no obligation to purchase any books and may cancel my subscription at any time. The free books and gift will be mine to keep in any case.

P3ZEE

Ms/Mrs/Miss/Mr ....Initials...............................
BLOCK CAPITALS PLEASE

Surname ....

Address ....

....

....Postcode.................................

Send this whole page to:
UK: FREEPOST CN81, Croydon, CR9 3WZ
EIRE: PO Box 4546, Kilcock, County Kildare (stamp required)

Offer valid in UK and Eire only and not available to current Reader Service subscribers to this series. We reserve the right to refuse an application and applicants must be aged 18 years or over. Only one application per household. Terms and prices subject to change without notice. Offer expires 31st October 2003. As a result of this application, you may receive offers from Harlequin Mills & Boon and other carefully selected companies. If you would prefer not to share in this opportunity please write to The Data Manager at the address above.

Mills & Boon® is a registered trademark owned by Harlequin Mills & Boon Limited.
Modern Romance™ is being used as a trademark.